PENGUIN BOOKS

THE DEATH AND LIFE OF DITH PRAN

Sydney H. Schanberg, a columnist for *The New York Times* on the problems and affairs of New York City, was born in 1934 in Clinton, Massachusetts, and attended Harvard College. In 1956 he was drafted into the Army, where he began his newspaper career as a writer for the 3rd Armored Division newspaper in Frankfurt, Germany. Mr. Schanberg joined *The Times* as a copy boy in 1959 and was promoted to reporter in 1960, later spending several years covering the state capital in Albany. He began reporting on Cambodia as a foreign correspondent in 1970, shortly after he took over *The Times*'s New Delhi bureau, and received several awards for his coverage of the India-Pakistan war in 1971. In 1973 he continued his coverage of Cambodia and Southeast Asia from the Singapore bureau, going to Phnom Penh for the last time in early January 1975. Mr. Schanberg's Cambodia coverage earned him the Pulitzer Prize in 1976 for international reporting "at great risk."

THE DEATH AND LIFE OF DITH PRAN

by SYDNEY H. SCHANBERG

ELISABETH SIFTON BOOKS   PENGUIN BOOKS

ELISABETH SIFTON BOOKS • PENGUIN BOOKS
Viking Penguin Inc., 40 West 23rd Street,
New York, New York 10010, U.S.A.
Penguin Books Ltd, Harmondsworth,
Middlesex, England
Penguin Books Australia Ltd, Ringwood,
Victoria, Australia
Penguin Books Canada Limited, 2801 John Street,
Markham, Ontario, Canada L3R 1B4
Penguin Books (N.Z.) Ltd, 182–190 Wairau Road,
Auckland 10, New Zealand

First published in simultaneous hardcover and paperback editions by Viking
and Penguin Books 1985
Published simultaneously in Canada
Reprinted 1985

ISBN 0 14 00.8457 6

Most of the text of this book appeared originally in the January 20, 1980,
issue of *The New York Times Sunday Magazine*.

Printed in the United States of America by
R.R. Donnelley & Sons, Harrisonburg, Virginia
Set in Times Roman

For my children, Jessica and Rebecca
and for Elizabeth
and for Bailey Ruth

FOREWORD

The story of Cambodia is a universal one—it is not a new thing that small countries and vulnerable peoples get abused by the large and powerful. But the awfulness of what happened in Cambodia should not be allowed to blur into a historical generality. This is why I am glad that this account, originally published as a long magazine article in *The New York Times,* is now a book. Books fade more slowly than newspaper pages.

It appears here as it was written, in 1980. Events since then have altered the details of Cambodia's existence, but the basic fact of life for these people has remained unchanged. The Cambodians are still everyone's pawns and are still suffering terribly.

It is my hope that this chronicle of the relationship and experiences of the two of us—an American and a Cambodian brought together by a war—will help provide a glimpse at this history.

Sydney H. Schanberg

CONTENTS

Foreword   vii
The Death and Life of Dith Pran   1
Epilogue   71

THE DEATH
AND LIFE OF
DITH PRAN

I began the search for my friend Dith Pran in April 1975. Unable to protect him when the Khmer Rouge troops ordered Cambodians to evacuate their cities, I had watched him disappear into the interior of Cambodia, which was to become a death camp for millions. Dith Pran had saved my life the day of the occupation, and the shadow of my failure to keep him safe—to do what he had done for me—was to follow me for four and a half years.

Then, on October 3, 1979, Dith Pran crossed the border to Thailand and freedom. This is a story of war and friendship, of the anguish of a ruined country, and of one man's will to live.

In July 1975—a few months after Pran and I had been forced apart on April 20—an American diplomat who had known Pran wrote me a consoling letter. The diplomat, who had served in Phnom Penh, knew the odds of anyone emerging safely from a country that was being transformed into a society of terror and purges and "killing fields." But he wrote: "Pran, I believe, is a survivor—in the Darwinian sense—and I think it only a matter of time before he seizes an available opportunity to slip across the border."

Pran is indeed a survivor. When he slipped across the border into Thailand, he was very thin, his teeth were rotting, and his hands shook from malnutrition—but he had not succumbed.

Pran's strength is returning and he wants the story told of what has happened, and is still happening, to his people. He wants to talk about the unthinkable statistic that Cambodia has become: an estimated two million or more people, out of a population of seven million in 1975, have been massacred or have died of starvation or disease.

I met Pran for the first time in 1972, two years after the war between the Khmer Rouge and the American-supported Lon Nol government had begun. I went to Cambodia that year after several months of helping cover a major offensive by Hanoi in South Vietnam for *The New York Times*. For some time, Pran had worked with Craig Whitney, our Saigon bureau chief, as his assistant on his occasional trips to Phnom Penh. When my plane touched down at Pochentong Airport on that September day, Pran had received my cable and was there to meet me.

His notebook was full of the things that had been happening since *The Times*'s last visit. A spacious suite with balcony was waiting for me at the Hotel Le Phnom, my press card and cable-filing permission had already been arranged for, and he had a list of valuable suggestions about what I should see and whom I should talk to. I felt immediately easy with him.

It is difficult to describe how a friendship grows, for it often grows from seemingly contradictory roots—mutual needs, overlapping dependencies, intense shared experiences, and even the inequality of status, with one serving the other.

Our bond grew in all these ways. Other reporters and television crews also vied for Pran's services, but more and more he politely turned them down and worked only for me. By the middle of 1973, his value to the paper now apparent, the foreign desk, at my urging, took Pran on as an official stringer with a monthly retainer. This took him completely out of circulation for other journalists, some of whom expressed their disappointment openly.

Pran and I realized early on that our ideas about the war were much the same. We both cared little about local or international politics or about military strategy. I had been drawn to the story by my perception of Cambodia as a nation pushed into the war by other powers, not in control of its destiny, being used callously as battle fodder, its agonies largely ignored as the world focused its attention on neighboring Vietnam. But what propelled both of us was the human impact—the ten-year-old orphans in uniforms, carrying rifles almost as tall as themselves; the amputees lying traumatized in filthy, overcrowded hospitals; the skeletal infants rasping and spitting as they died while you watched in the all-too-few malnutrition clinics; and the sleepless, unpaid soldiers taking heavy fire at the front lines, depending on the "magic" amulets they wore around their necks while their generals took siestas after long lunches several miles behind the fighting. And then, always, the refugees. While White House policy-makers were recommending only a few million dollars for relief aid, as compared with somewhere around one billion dollars in military aid, on the ground that there was really no major refugee problem in Cambodia, Pran was taking me to the jammed and underfed refugee camps and to the dirt roads not far from Phnom Penh where villagers were streaming away from the fighting, leaving their homes and rice fields behind.

We were not always depressed by the war, however, because the opposite side of depression is exhilaration—the highs of staying alive and of getting big stories. And he and I covered many big stories. Like the time in 1973 when an American B-52 bomber, through an error by the crew in activating its computerized homing system, dropped twenty or more tons of bombs on the heavily populated Mekong town of Neak Luong, thirty-eight miles southeast of Phnom Penh. About 150 people were killed and more than 250 wounded. The mortified

American Embassy played down the destruction ("I saw one stick of bombs through the town," said the air attaché, "but it was no great disaster") and then tried to keep reporters from getting there. They succeeded the first day, barring us from helicopters and river patrol boats, but on the second, Pran, his competitiveness boiling as keenly as mine, managed, through bribes and cajoling, to sneak us aboard a patrol boat. We brought back the first full story of the tragedy.

But first we were put under house arrest for one night by the military in Neak Luong—we always believed the orders came from the Americans. We spent the night in a house with some of the survivors. They stayed up all night, listening for the sound of airplanes, in dread that another "friendly" plane would rain death on them again.

On our way back up the river, on another patrol boat, the crew was less interested in getting us back to Phnom Penh in time to file before the cable office shut down for the night than in scouring the riverbanks for Communist machine-gun and rocket nests. Every time they thought they spotted something—be it driftwood or the real thing—they turned the craft toward the shore and opened up with their .50-caliber machine gun.

We were going to be too late if this continued, so Pran told them—on my frantic instructions—that he would double the bribes if only they would ignore their military targets and move at full speed to Phnom Penh. They understood our motives not at all—I'm sure they regarded me as deranged—but their official salary was a pittance, and they did as they were asked.

Days and nights spent like this were what drew Pran and me together.

I pause here to say that this chronicle, of all the stories I have written as a journalist, has become the hardest for me to pull out of my insides. To describe a relationship such as Pran's and mine demands candor and frankness about self, not romantic memories. I feel exposed and vulnerable. I also wonder nervously what he will think when he reads this. As I write, there is a tension pain under my right shoulder blade, the same pain I felt in April 1975, in the final days before the fall of Phnom Penh, after the American Embassy had been evacuated. We ran chaotically around the city and its perimeter every day, trying to piece together what was happening and how close the Communists were. Our nights were spent at the cable office—I typed while Pran urged the Teletype operators to keep going and push the copy out. Our two drivers, Hea and Sarun, were there, too, bringing me wet washcloths and glasses of weak tea to keep me awake. The city's power was off and there was no air-conditioning. When I would begin to slump, Sarun would bring me back by rubbing my shoulders and pulling on my ears, a traditional Cambodian massage.

Among the papers strewn about me now is a picture of Sarun, shirtless and sweating, pulling on my ears. It is not easy for me to look at that picture. Sarun is dead now, killed in 1977 when the Khmer Rouge, for some unknown reason, decided to execute all the men in his village. Sarun's wife later met Pran in Siem Reap province and told him that Sarun had cried out horribly, pleading for mercy as they dragged him off, his hands bound tightly behind him.

My mind searches for happier times. I remember our visit to Battambang in 1974, when, over a tasty fish dinner, Pran and I smoked pot, he for the first time, and then went gamboling through the unlighted streets of the town, astonishing soldiers at checkpoints as we bayed at the moon. I remember the time in late 1973 when, frayed and needing a breather, we flew to the seaport resort of Kompong Som and played on the beaches for three days. I can see Pran in the water, giggling as he groped among the rocks, looking for the sweet crabs that lived in abundance there.

But as I wander mentally over the landscape of those war years, starker memories swarm, disjointed, out of sequence, clamoring for precedence.

In 1973, Thomas O. Enders, an arrogant protégé of Secretary of State Henry A. Kissinger, became acting ambassador in Phnom Penh, taking over from Emory Swank, who had refused to supervise the heavy American bombing, and who was relegated by Kissinger to a State Department dustbin because he no longer had any stomach for this futile war. Enders, who made no secret of the low regard in which he held the Cambodians for their inability to defeat the Communist army, had no such reservations. According to participants, he ran the morning bombing meetings at the embassy, where targets were chosen for the daily carpet bombing by the giant B-52s, with spirit and relish.

Enders also became known around Phnom Penh for remarks that some listeners considered openly callous and racist. He would ask, rhetorically, at cocktail parties, diplomatic dinners, and press briefings why the Cambodians did not seem to care as much about human life as we Westerners. If they did care, he posited, they would rise up in anger over the terrorist rocket attacks that were killing innocent victims daily in the capital, and march out into the countryside to smite the Communist army.

Pran had heard about Enders's remarks, but we had not discussed them. Finally, fed up, I asked Pran one day what he would reply to Enders if the diplomat asked him, "Do Khmers care less about the death of their loved ones than other people do?"

Pran lowered his head for several minutes. Then softly he said: "It's not true. You have seen for yourself the suffering. The only difference, maybe, is that with Cambodians the grief leaves the face quickly, but it goes inside and stays there for a long time."

In 1975, the Khmer Rouge rockets began falling on the neighborhood where Pran lived with his wife and children. One morning he was late coming to work. He explained that just as he was leaving the house, a rocket crashed into the house of a neighbor. A six-year-old girl was severely wounded. Her stomach was hanging out. Pran raced her to the hospital in his car, her mother screaming all the way. The child did not survive.

Another visit to Neak Luong, in 1975, is also part of the mosaic. By this time, the strategic river port is surrounded by the Khmer Rouge, who are bombarding it with rockets and mortars. Thirty thousand refugees are trapped there. Food is short. The gravely wounded are so numerous and the medivac helicopters so few that some of the victims are asking to be killed quickly rather than be allowed to lie there and die slowly in pain. Pran and I fly in by helicopter on January 14; the meadow where we land is filled with the dead and dying. Every fifteen minutes or so, another shell screams down and another half-dozen or so are killed or wounded. Inside the tiny military infirmary, an eleven-year-old boy has just expired on the blood-slick floor. In the bedlam, no one has time to cover him or even to close his staring eyes.

When we arrive back in Phnom Penh, I am frantic to get my film to Saigon, where it can be radiophotoed to New York. There's only one more flight today, an American Embassy plane, leaving in half an hour. While I run to the airline terminal building to call the embassy for permission to send film on the plane, I send Pran to the tarmac with the film, in case the plane comes early, so he can try to wheedle it aboard. When I return, having got permission, Pran has disappeared. None of the Americans on the tarmac—military men in civilian clothes responsible for supervising the delivery of United States military supplies to Phnom Penh—will tell me what has happened to him. With five minutes to go before takeoff, I spot Pran waving at me from behind a warehouse a couple hundred yards away. I recover the film from him, just manage to get it on the plane, and then walk back to ask him what in the world happened.

He tells me that an American colonel ordered him off the airport, citing security reasons. Washington contends that it has no advisers here and that the Cambodians are running their own war, yet an American officer orders a Cambodian off a Cambodian airport.

"The Americans are king here now," Pran says dejectedly. "It's his land, not mine anymore."

I ask the embassy for an explanation and for an apology to Pran. We get neither.

Our lives proceeded in this fashion—from one intense experience to another, an unnatural existence by the standards of normal life, but perfectly natural when living inside a continuous crisis. We broke our tension—we had to, for psychic survival, to push away the bloody images—with good food, laughter that was often too loud, and occasionally an evening of carousing and smoking pot, which was plentiful and cheap in the central market. (Pran abstained after his howling at the stars in Battambang.)

My trips to Cambodia from Singapore, where I was based,

became more frequent and my stays longer. I was becoming part of the war, and it was placing bad strains on my wife, Janice, and my two young daughters, Jessica and Rebecca, and on my relationships with each of them.

Once, returning to Singapore after a three-month tour in Cambodia, I noticed that Jessica, then only five, was very shy and distant with me. I tried to draw her out, asking if there was something wrong. "No, Daddy," she said uncomfortably, having difficulty finding the words without offending me, "I love you. But I keep losing you. Just when I'm getting to know you again, I lose you."

But I kept going back to Phnom Penh; my obsession with the story was filling my life. Pran, too, was hooked, for some of my reasons but also for some very personal ones of his own. He had no background in journalism when the war began, but as his skills improved and his interest in the craft grew, he began to see in journalism a way to reveal his people's plight.

Born on September 27, 1942, Pran was raised in a middle-class family with three brothers and two sisters in the township of Siem Reap, in the northwestern part of the country, near the famed Angkor temples. His father was a senior public-works official, who supervised the building of roads in the area. Pran went through high school there, learning French in the classroom and English on his own at home. After high school, in 1960, he got a job as an interpreter in Khmer, the Cambodian language, for the United States Military Assistance Group then in Cambodia. When Cambodia broke relations with Washington in 1965, charging that American troops had launched attacks from South Vietnam on Cambodian border villages, the Americans left and Pran got a job as an interpreter for the British film crew that was producing *Lord Jim*.

After that, he became a receptionist at Cambodia's best-known tourist hotel, Auberge Royale des Temples, situated just opposite the main entrance to the Angkor complex. Tourism ended with the beginning of the war in 1970, and Pran went to Phnom Penh with his wife, Ser Moeun, and their children to find work as a guide and interpreter for foreign journalists.

As the war dragged on and conditions deteriorated, I drove Pran very hard. I was driven, so I drove him. As always, I pushed him to go a little faster, get a little more done, interview a few more people. When, for example, the cable line out of Phnom Penh would go down, as it did frequently, I would send him over to the cable office to try to coax and bribe the operators into doing something special for us to get it working again. I would raise my voice every time some obstacle arose that could impede my getting a story out, telling him to get the problem resolved, even when I knew that in a country whose communications system was as primitive as Cambodia's, there was often little he could do.

He almost never complained or demurred. He says he never got angry at me, although I'm convinced there were times when he dearly wanted to bounce a chair off my head. He insists he accepted my relentless behavior as merely an attempt to teach him how to succeed as a journalist. "I never got angry," he says, "because I understand your heart. I also understand that you are a man who wants everything to succeed."

Pran was a survivor even then. He also tended to give me heroic qualities, to make me bigger than life—as I am perhaps doing to him now.

There was one day, however, when he did eventually reveal his annoyance. We had interviewed the prime minister, In Tam. Pran's translation of his remarks, which were in Khmer, was literal, and I was looking for the subtleties that would reveal the prime minister's intent. Pran first gave one meaning and then a different one, and we began to have a royal argument. I demanded to know what Pran thought In Tam's meaning had really been; I wanted the whole truth. Finally he retaliated. "I can't tell you the whole truth—I can only tell you eighty percent," he snapped. "Twenty percent I have to keep for myself."

My persona came to have a wider audience. I was dubbed "Ankalimir" by other Cambodian assistants in the press corps and employees at the Hotel Le Phnom, who had become accustomed to my outbursts. Ankalimir, in Khmer legend, was an ogre who went around cutting off the fingers of people who annoyed him. Until he got to his hundredth finger, which was his mother's. She was having none of this. She told him he'd been a bad man and it was time for him to reform. And he did. So dramatically did he change that he eventually was transformed into an enlightened disciple of Buddha's.

I was the man, my Cambodian friends explained, who made a lot of bad noises in the beginning but at bottom was a good person. I liked the ending and accepted the nickname as comradely, if critical, flattery.

On the day of the United States Embassy evacuation—April 12, 1975—all the Americans at the hotel, mostly newsmen, left the premises early in the morning. The employees thought all of us had left the city on Marine helicopters and, feeling abandoned with the Communists closing in on the city, became desolate. A few of us had decided to stay, however, and I was the first to walk back into the hotel at noontime. The receptionists and room boys came to life, jumping to their feet. "Ankalimir is still here," one shouted. Perhaps these gracious men took heart from my presence, as if I had some special information that we would all be safe when the Khmer Rouge came.

That evacuation day remains, paradoxically, both clear and muddled in my mind. What I do remember is Joe Lelyveld, then *The Times*'s Hong Kong bureau chief, who has come in to help with the coverage in the final weeks, banging on my door at 7 that morning.

He tells me that this is it, the embassy is leaving, we have to be there with our bags by 8:30, the gates close at 9:30. My first thought, utterly irrational, is that I can't possibly pack in time. My next thought is an equally irrational wish that it's only a test run, because I don't really want to leave.

Eventually I have a lucid thought. I have to talk to Pran. We had worked until 3 in the morning and he's probably still sleeping. First, I speed to the embassy to convince myself it's the real thing. It is, so I race back to the hotel, send a messenger for Pran, and, as a contingency, I pack. I guess this means that I am not going to make a final decision until I can look into his face.

When he arrives, I tell him quickly about the evacuation and ask him if he wants to leave. Knowing this day was coming, we had discussed the options several times before and agreed that if we felt in no direct danger, we would stay. Though we have little time, his face is calm. He knows I want to stay, and he says he doesn't see any immediate risk and therefore no reason we should leave now. He says he wants to stay to cover the story. We reinforce each other's compulsions and desires. He is as obsessed as I am with seeing the story to the end.

But he adds that with rockets falling on his neighborhood, he wants to evacuate his wife and children. I had already taken the precaution of getting the approval of a sympathetic senior embassy official, Robert Keeley, to accept any Cambodian friends I might bring to the embassy on the day of the evacuation. I send Pran rushing home to collect his family in his aging green Renault, and I go to wait for them at the embassy, now surrounded and secured by Marines in full battle dress.

In the sky, the helicopters swarm like wasps, heading in and out of the landing zone nearby, taking evacuees to the aircraft carrier USS *Okinawa* in the Gulf of Siam, which will then head for Thailand. A steady stream of foreigners, Cambodians, and embassy officials arrive at the building and pass through a special metal door. Brown tags with their names on them are placed around their necks, and they are then moved to the flatbed trucks that will take them to the landing zone. Some have tears in their eyes, but most mask their feelings. Some Cambodians who try to get into the embassy have no authorization and are turned away. One distraught man slips a note in English through a crack in the metal door. It reads: "Will you please bring me and my family out of the country?" But the man has no connections at the embassy. "Give it back," growls a nervous American colonel, "give it back." The note is passed back through the slit. No one inside ever sees the face of the man making the appeal.

At 9:20—with only ten minutes to spare—Pran drives up with his family. As his wife and their four children are loaded onto the last truck, an Army military attaché who is going out on the same truck tries to persuade us to come with them. When he realizes our decision to stay is final, he holds out his automatic rifle and asks, "Don't you want something for protection?" I tell him that I am touched by his offer, but that I'm all thumbs and I'd probably blow off a toe if I tried to use it. He keeps holding out the rifle to me, even as the truck goes out the embassy's back gate.

At 11:13, the last helicopter takes off. The dust on the landing zone, a soccer field, settles. The skies are silent.

Very suddenly the city takes on a strange, new atmosphere—a feeling of emptiness, if that's possible in a refugee-crowded capital of two and a half million. The Americans were the last power base. Now, it's like having the city to ourselves; we're on our own for everything. We don't admit it to each other, but it's more than a little eerie. We begin to feel a heightened kinship with the Westerners who have stayed—more than seven hundred French colonials, a score of mostly French and Swedish journalists, and another score of international relief officials. There are also five other Americans, ranging from a freelance photographer to an alcoholic airline mechanic who has drunkenly slept through the evacuation calls.

Much of what happened over the next five days—until the Khmer Rouge came—was reported at that time in *The New York Times*. Pran and I sped around the city and its perimeter every day in our two rented Mercedes-Benzes, trying to visit every front line, every hospital, every possible government official—to put together as clear a picture as possible of the increasingly chaotic situation. One thing was certain: the enemy circle around Phnom Penh was tightening.

These were long, frenetic, sweaty days. Our lives—and our options—had been reduced to necessities. We carried basic needs with us—typewriters and typing paper in the cars, survival kits (passport, money, change of shirt and underwear, camera, film, extra notebooks, soap, toothbrush) over our shoulders, Pran's in a knapsack, mine in a blue Pan Am bag.

Although I kept my room at the hotel, we rarely stopped there. We spent most of our nights at the cable office, filing stories—or trying to. The main transmission tower, in a suburb called Kambol, was eventually overrun, and the last remaining transmitter was an ancient Chinese-made contraption that kept overheating and going dead. We caught only a couple of hours of sleep each night, on straw mats on the cable office floor. There was little time to bathe or change clothes, but since we all smelled alike, no one took offense.

There was also little time to reflect on what might happen when the Khmer Rouge took the city. Our decision to stay was founded on our belief—perhaps, looking back, it was more a devout wish or hope—that when they won their victory, they would have what they wanted and would end the terrorism and brutal behavior we had written so often about. We all wanted to believe that, since both sides were Khmers, they would find a route to reconciliation. Most of the high officials in the government put their lives on this belief and stayed behind too. Those who were caught were executed.

On April 14, the Khmer Rouge begin their final push, driving on the airport, one of the city's last lines of defense.

Inside the capital, there remains a strange disconnection from the reality that is such a short distance away. Some of the Frenchmen who have stayed behind, believing that as old residents and relics of the colonial past their lives will not be disrupted, are playing chess by the hotel pool. In a nearby street, a driver leans on the fender of his Land Rover, a mirror in one hand and tweezers in the other, pulling stray hairs from his chin. Government employees laugh and joke as they go through their regular morning marching exercises on the grass outside their buildings—part of a national preparedness program. For two days, the government news agency carries nothing on the evacuation of the Americans, but it has a long story on the death of the entertainer Josephine Baker. The government radio announces the appointment of a new Minister of State for Industry, Mines and Tourism. A delicious *petit poussin* is served in the hotel restaurant, but an American patron complains because the hotel has run out of ice and he objects to drinking his Pepsi warm.

This surrealism is to come to an end on the morning of April 17, a Thursday, when the new rulers march into the anxious city. On the night of April 16 it is clear that the collapse of Phnom Penh is only hours away. Enormous fires from the battles that ring the very edge of the city turn the night sky orange. The last government planes—single-engine propeller craft diving low over the treetops—futilely try to halt the Communist advance with their final bombs. Refugees by the thousands swarm into the heart of the capital, bringing their oxcarts, their meager belongings, and their frightened bedlam. Deserting government soldiers are among them.

Pran turns to me and says: "It's finished, it's finished." And as we look at each other, we see on each other's faces for the first time the nagging anxiety about what is going to happen to us.

We spend that final night filing stories from the cable office, as artillery shells crash down periodically a few hundred yards away. The line goes dead just before 6 a.m. on April 17; two of my pages still have not been sent. I am annoyed and complain edgily to the morning crew chief, badgering him to do something to get the line restored. Within a moment, I feel as foolish and contrite as it is possible for a man to feel. The telephone rings. It is a message for the crew chief. One of his children has been killed and his wife critically wounded by an artillery shell that has fallen on his home in the southern section of Phnom Penh. As his colleagues offer words of solace, he holds his face under control, his lips pressed tightly together. He puts on his tie and his jacket and he leaves, without ever saying a word, for the hospital where his wife is dying.

We leave the cable office and take a short swing by car to the northern edge of the city. The sun is rising but it offers no comfort. Soldiers and refugees are trudging in from the northern defense line, which has collapsed. Fires are burning along the line of retreat.

By the time we reach the hotel, the retreat can be clearly seen from my third-floor balcony, and small-arms fire can be heard. Soldiers are stripping off their uniforms and changing into civilian clothes. At 6:30 a.m., I write in my notebook: "The city is falling."

Pran is listening to the government radio, which is playing martial music and gives no hint of the collapse. The day before, the prime minister, Long Boret, had sent a virtual surrender offer, via Red Cross radio, to the Khmer Rouge side; it asked only for assurances of no reprisals against people and organizations who had worked on the government side. Prince Norodom Sihanouk, as titular head of the Khmer Rouge, immediately rejected the offer from his exile in Peking. The government radio went off the air last night without mentioning the truce offer; it said only that the military situation "is boiling hotter and hotter" and quoted government leaders as "determined to fight to the last drop of our blood."

Now, as Pran glues his ear to the radio, I decide that, not having bathed in two days, I shall shower and change clothes. "If we're going to meet the new rulers of Phnom Penh today," I tell him jokingly, "I'd better look my best." He laughs, amused at another irrational act by the man whose first thought on the day the Americans left was that he didn't have time to pack. I emerge from my shave and shower feeling halfway recycled. At 7:20 a.m., the Khmer Rouge break in on the radio to announce: "We are ready to welcome you."

It is the apprehensive population of Phnom Penh that does the welcoming—hanging white flags, fashioned from bed sheets, from windows and rooftops and on government gunboats on the Tonle Sap River and the Mekong. The crews of the armored personnel carriers in the streets outside the hotel stick bouquets of yellow allamanda flowers in their headlights.

The first units of Communist troops seem friendly and celebratory. They are wearing clean black pajama uniforms and look remarkably uncalloused and unscarred. It soon becomes clear that they are not the real Khmer Rouge—we never did learn who they were, maybe misguided students trying to share in the "revolution," maybe part of a desperate plot by the government to confuse and subvert the Khmer Rouge—but within hours they and their leader are disarmed and under arrest and the genuine Khmer Rouge take over and begin ruthlessly driving the people of the city into the countryside. Most of the soldiers are teenagers, which is startling. They are universally grim, robotlike, brutal. Weapons drip from them like fruit from trees—grenades, pistols, rifles, rockets.

During the first confused hours of the Communist victory, when it looks as if our belief in reconciliation is a possibility, Pran and I and Jon Swain of *The Sunday Times* of London, who has been traveling with us, decide to chance a walk to the cable office. The transmitter is still out of order, so we can send no copy, but a beaming Teletype operator chortles at us, *"C'est la paix! C'est la paix!"*

Outside, at 10:40 a.m., we have our first conversation with an insurgent soldier. He says he is twenty-five years old, has been five years in the "movement" and has had ten years of schooling. He is traveling on a bicycle and is wearing green government fatigues over his black pajamas. The government-unit patches have been torn off. He has a Mao cap and shower sandals, and around his neck he wears a cheap, small pair of field glasses. Like all the others we meet later, he refuses to give his name or rank. We guess he is an officer or sergeant.

Will the Khmer take revenge and kill a lot of people? I ask Pran to ask him in Khmer. "Those who have done corrupt things will definitely have to be punished," he says.

Pran tries to get him to relax and at one point does evoke a small smile from this man from another planet. It is one of the few smiles I will see on a Khmer Rouge face for the two weeks I am to be under their control. I offer him cigarettes and oranges. He refuses, saying that he is not allowed to accept gifts. I ask him if he can give gifts: what about his Mao cap, would he give it to me as a souvenir? He refuses coldly. The smile is gone. He pedals off.

After a breakfast of Pepsi-Cola at a restaurant whose French proprietor is glad for company but who has no other food, we walk back to the hotel and decide it is still safe to move around. So we drive to the biggest civilian hospital—Preah Keth Mealea—to get some idea of casualties. Al Rockoff, an American freelance photographer, has joined us. Only a handful of doctors have reported for duty. People are bleeding to death on the corridor floors. A Khmer Rouge soldier, caked with blood, is getting plasma from one of the few nurses who have showed up, but he is nevertheless dying of severe head and stomach wounds. All he can manage to whisper, over and over, is, "Water, water." A few yards away, hospital aides are trying to mop some of the blood off the floor. They mop carefully around three stiffening corpses.

We can stand to look at these scenes no longer, so we depart. But as we get into our car and start to leave the compound, some heavily armed Khmer Rouge soldiers charge in through the main gate. Shouting and angry, they wave us out of the car, put guns to our heads and stomachs, and order us to put our hands over our heads. I instinctively look at Pran for guidance. We have been in difficult situations before, but this is the first time I have ever seen raw fear on his face. He tells me, stammering, to do everything they say. I am shaking. I think we're going to be killed right there. But Pran, having somehow composed himself, starts pleading with them. His hands still over his head, he tries to convince them we are not their enemy, merely foreign newsmen covering their victory.

They take everything—our car, cameras, typewriters, radio, knapsacks—and push us into an armored personnel carrier, a kind of light tank that carries troops in its belly, which they have captured from the government army.

We all get in—three journalists and our driver, Sarun—except for Pran. We hear him continuing his entreaties in Khmer outside. We naturally think he is trying to get away, arguing against getting into this vehicle. Most of my thoughts are jumbled and incoherent, but I remember thinking, For God's sake, Pran, get inside. Maybe there's some chance this way, but if you go on arguing, they'll shoot you down in the street.

Finally, he climbs in, the rear door and top hatch are slammed shut, and the armored car starts to rumble forward. After a few minutes of chilled silence, Sarun turns to me and in French asks me if I know what Pran was doing outside the vehicle. I say no, since the talk was in Khmer. Sarun tells me that Pran, far from trying to get away, was doing the opposite—trying to talk his way into the armored car. The Khmer Rouge had told him to leave, they didn't want him, only the Americans and "the big people." He knew we had no chance without him, so he argued not to be separated from us, offering, in effect, to forfeit his own life on the chance that he might save ours.

As the armored car moves through the city, it becomes an oven. Sweat starts pouring off us as we stare at one another's frightened countenances. The vehicle suddenly stops. Two Cambodian men are pushed inside. They are dressed in civilian clothes, but Pran recognizes them as military men who have taken off their uniforms to try to escape detection. One of them, a burly man with a narrow mustache, wearing a T-shirt and jeans, reaches over and tries to shove his wallet into my back pocket. He explains in whispered French that he is an officer and must hide his identity. I tell him it is useless to hide anything on me because we are all in the same predicament. Pran takes the wallet and stuffs it under some burlap sacks we are sitting on. The officer's companion, a shorter, leaner man with a crew cut, dressed in a flowered shirt and brown trousers, has a small ivory Buddha on a gold chain around his neck. He puts the Buddha in his mouth and begins to pray—a Cambodian Buddhist ritual to summon good fortune against imminent danger. His behavior is contagious. I take from my pocket a yellow silk rose that my daughter Jessica had given me two weeks earlier when I had taken a five-day breather in Bangkok with my family, knowing the fall of Phnom Penh was near. I had cut off the wire stem and carried it in my pocket ever since, as my personal amulet. Sweat has turned it into a sodden and scruffy lump. I clutch it hard in my right fist for luck.

Looking across at Jon Swain, I see in his eyes what must also be in mine—a certainty that we are to be executed. Trying to preserve my dignity and to get that terrible look off his face, I hold out the rose and say: "Look, Jon, I've got Jessica's good-luck rose with me. Nothing can really happen to us." He forces a wan grimace; I know he thinks I am crazy.

Meanwhile, Pran is keeping up his pleading with the driver

of the armored car, telling him that we are not soldiers or politicians or anyone hostile to the Khmer Rouge. No one here is American, he insists, they are all French, they are only newsmen. Whatever meager words we exchange among ourselves are in French. Rockoff speaks no French, so we run our hands across our lips in a sealing motion to let him know he should keep his mouth shut.

Suddenly, after a forty-minute ride, the vehicle stops and the rear door clangs open. We are ordered to get out. As we move, crouching through the door, we see two Khmer Rouge soldiers, their rifles on their hips pointing directly at us. Behind them is a sandy riverbank that slopes down to the Tonle Sap River. Rockoff and I exchange the briefest of fear-struck glances. We are thinking the same thing—they're going to do it here and roll us down the bank into the river.

But we climb out, like zombies, and no shots are yet fired. Pran resumes his pleas, searching out a soldier who looks like an officer. For a solid hour he keeps this up—appealing, cajoling, begging for our lives. The officer sends a courier on a motorbike to some headquarters in the center of the city. We wait, still frozen but trying to hope, as Pran continues talking. Finally, the courier returns, more talk—and then, miraculously, the rifles are lowered. We are permitted to have a drink of water. I look at Pran and he allows himself a cautious smile. He's done it, I think, he's pulled it off.

Strangely, in the surge of relief, my first thought is of my notebooks, which were in my airline bag, confiscated when we were seized. I feel more than a little silly to be thinking now of pieces of paper. But my sense of loss is overwhelming—the notebooks hold all my thoughts, everything I had observed, for the last several months.

We are still under guard, but everything has relaxed. They

now let us move into the shade of a concrete approach to a bridge blown up by sappers early in the war. We watch jubilant Communist soldiers rolling by in trucks loaded with looted cloth, wine, liquor, cigarettes, and soft drinks. They scatter some of the booty to the soldiers at the bridge. We also watch civilian refugees leaving Phnom Penh in a steady stream— our first solid evidence that they are driving the city's entire population of more than two million into the countryside to join their "peasant revolution." As the refugees plod along, the soldiers take watches and radios from them.

Our captors offer us soft drinks. One of them toys with me. He holds out a bottle of orange soda, and when I reach for it, he pulls it back. Finally I say, "Thank you very much," in Khmer. Having made his point, that I am his subject, in his control, he hands me the bottle, grinning.

At 3:30 p.m. we are released. Suddenly a jeep drives up, and many of our belongings are in it—including the airline bag. Sheepishly, I ask Pran if he thinks he can get it back. He sees nothing unusual in the request and immediately begins bargaining. A few minutes later, a Khmer Rouge soldier, after haphazardly groping through its insides, hands me the bag. In it, with the notebooks, is a money belt holding nine thousand dollars and my American passport, which, if they had bothered to look at it, could have given me away. Our hired 1967 Mercedes-Benz and my camera, among other valuables, were kept as booty.

As we move off, I look back. The two men who shared the armored car with us are still under guard. The smaller man still has the Buddha in his mouth, having never stopped praying. There is no doubt in our minds that they are marked for execution.

Much later, I ask Pran about the extraordinary thing he had

done, about why he had argued his way into that armored car when he could have run away. He explains in a quiet voice: "You don't speak Khmer, and I cannot let you go off and get killed without someone talking to them and trying to get them to understand. Even if I get killed, I have to first try to say something to them. Because you and I are together. I was very scared, yes, because in the beginning I thought they were going to kill us, but my heart said I had to try this. I understand you and know your heart well. You would do the same thing for me."

The rest of that day is an adrenaline blur, a lifetime crammed into a few hours. We see friends going off to certain death, families pleading with us to save them as we professed our helplessness, roads awash with people being swept out of the city like human flotsam. Some are the severely wounded from the hospitals, who are being pushed in their beds, serum bottles still attached to their bodies.

After our release, we head for the Information Ministry because earlier Khmer Rouge radio broadcasts have called on all high officials of the defeated government to report there. We find about fifty prisoners standing outside the building, guarded by wary Khmer Rouge troops. They also begin to guard us as we approach the men who appear to be their leaders and seek to interview them. Among the prisoners are cabinet ministers and generals, including Brigadier General Lon Non, younger brother of Marshal Lon Nol, who went into exile some weeks before. Lon Non, considered one of the most corrupt men in Cambodia, is smoking a pipe and trying to look untroubled. He says calmly to us, "I don't know what will happen to me."

A Khmer Rouge official, probably a general, though like all the others his uniform bears no markings of rank, addresses the group with a bullhorn, telling them that they will be dealt with fairly. He asks for their cooperation, saying, "There will be no reprisals." The prisoners' strained faces suggest they do not believe him. (Whether this entire group was killed is not known, but Lon Non's execution is confirmed a short time later.)

Three Cambodian women suddenly walk into this tense scene. They go straight to the leader and tell him they wish to offer their help. They are officials of the Cambodian Red Cross— middle-aged patrician ladies dedicated to good works. They do not seem to understand what is happening. The leader smiles and thanks them for coming. They depart as incongruously as they came.

The Khmer Rouge leader, who seems no older than thirty-five, then turns to talk to us and a few French newsmen who have joined our group. He is polite but says very little. Pran serves as interpreter. When we ask if we will be allowed to cable stories to our publications, he says, "We will resolve all problems in their proper order." He also volunteers "our thanks to the American people, who have helped us from the beginning."

He suggests to Pran that the foreign newsmen stay at the Information Ministry to be registered. Pran, sensing trouble, declines politely and motions discreetly to us to leave. We slip away, smiling as broadly as we can.

Just then, the prime minister of the old government, Long Boret, arrives in a car driven by his wife. He is a courageous man who could have left with the Americans but stayed behind to try to work out a peaceful transition of power. He has failed and he looks wretched. His eyes are puffed. He stares at the ground. He is one of the seven "traitors" specifically marked by the Khmer Rouge for execution, and he knows what faces him now. I want to get away, but I feel I must say something to him, and Pran understands. I take Long Boret's hands and tell him what a brave thing he has done for his country and that I admire him for it.

Pran takes his hands, too. I feel dehumanized at not being able to do anything but offer a few words. Long Boret tries to respond but cannot. Finally he mumbles, "Thank you." And we must leave him.

As we head back to the hotel on foot, a gray Mercedes approaches us and stops. The driver jumps out and comes toward me, haggard and stuttering, holding some pieces of paper. It is Ang Kheao, a gentle middle-aged man who used to teach at the university and sometimes did translations of documents for me. For the past week, I have had him monitoring government radio broadcasts. His large family is jammed into the car; like everyone else, they are leaving the city under the Khmer Rouge orders of evacuation. It is hard to believe, but in the midst of chaos, with his family in jeopardy, Ang Kheao has kept on working to complete his assignment.

I look at the papers he hands me—it is his translation of the final broadcast of the defeated government, transmitted around noontime. The government announcer had started reading a message saying that talks between the two sides had begun, when a Khmer Rouge official in the booth with him interrupted to say, harshly: "We did not come here to talk. We enter Phnom Penh not for negotiation, but as conquerors."

Ang Kheao and I say goodbye as if in a ritual. I pay him for his services and offer him my meaningless wishes for good luck. He wishes me good health in return and drives off toward the northwest, up Highway 5. Another friend I shall probably never see again.

It is exactly 5:20 p.m. when we reach the Hotel Le Phnom.

It is deserted. Insurgent troops sit in a truck outside the gate, their rocket launchers trained ominously on the building. I run up to the only foreigner in sight, a Swedish Red Cross official standing on the front steps. "What's going on?" I ask. Peering at me through his monocle, he says calmly: "They gave us half an hour to empty the hotel. They gave no reason." "When did they give you that half hour?" I ask nervously. "Twenty-five minutes ago," he replies.

So the overflowing hotel, which the Red Cross had tried to turn into a protected international zone, is no longer a sanctuary, and we must fall back on the contingency plan that has been worked out among the foreigners remaining in Phnom Penh, which is to seek refuge in the French Embassy about a half-mile away.

I have five minutes to collect the loose clothes I left behind as dispensable. Jon Swain, his hotel key confiscated by the Khmer Rouge with his other belongings, will now need them. Also in my room—and more important—is a cupboard full of survival rations, collected judiciously for just such an event: canned meat, tins of fruit and juice, sardines. While I'm in the bedroom throwing the clothes into a suitcase, I yell at Rockoff to empty the cupboard. He packs up a few things— a can of Dinty Moore beef stew, a jar of Lipton's powdered iced tea, and a tin of wafers—but he completely ignores everything else, including a fruitcake and a large jar of chunky peanut butter. In the days ahead, when we are often hungry, we rag him good-naturedly—but continually—about this lapse.

We are the last ones out of the building, running. The Red Cross has abandoned several vehicles in the hotel yard after removing the keys. We have too much to carry, so we throw our gear in the back of one of their Toyota vans, put it in neutral, and start pushing it up Monivong Boulevard toward the French Embassy. The broad avenue is awash with refugees, bent under sacks of belongings, marching into the unknown, their eyes hurt with the knowledge that, being soft city people, the trek into the interior will certainly kill many of them.

In the tidal crush, people have lost shoes and sandals, and footwear litters the street. Cars with flat tires stand abandoned in the middle of the road. Clouds of smoke from the final battles wreathe the city. Coming from the north along Monivong is a fresh, heavily armed battalion, marching in single file. As we pass, we eye one another like people from different universes.

At the French Embassy, there is pandemonium. The gates are shut and locked to prevent the mob from surging in, but people by the dozens, including Cambodians, are coming in anyway—passing their children over the tall iron-spiked fence, then hurling their belongings over and finally climbing over themselves. We do the same.

Entering the compound, we are immediately segregated racially by the French officials. Westerners are allowed inside the embassy's four buildings. (About eight hundred eventually gather in the compound.) Cambodians and other Asians must camp on the grass outside. A French Embassy official with a guard dog bars me from taking Pran and our two drivers, Hea and Sarun, and their families inside our building, the Salle de Reception; we sneak them in after dark. At about 9 p.m., a report sweeps the compound that the Khmer Rouge are ordering all Cambodians out of the embassy and into the countryside. The five hundred Cambodians outside the embassy buildings sit up all night in anxiety, ready to run and hide, afraid to go to sleep. In a few days, this report will become a reality, and the Cambodians will indeed be pushed out.

Talks are begun between the Khmer Rouge and our side (embassy officials and representatives of the United Nations and other international agencies), but our basic requests—for delivery of food from the outside world, for an air evacuation of everyone in the compound—are curtly rejected. The Khmer Rouge make it clear that we and our requests are not merely unimportant but irrelevant. At one point they say that the "indispensable" evacuation of Phnom Penh "does not concern you." More disquieting, even though France has recognized their government, they reject the international convention that the embassy is foreign territory and therefore a place of asylum, inviolate and protected. They enter the compound at will, taking away people they consider "high enemies," including Sirik Matak, a Cambodian general and former prime minister. In a funereal drizzle he walks out the gate into Khmer Rouge custody. "I am not afraid," he says, as he is led to the back of a flatbed garbage truck, his back straight and his head high. "I am ready to account for my actions." He is executed soon after.

From our small window on their revolution—the embassy's front gate—we can see glimpses of their "peasant revolution." There is no doubt that the Khmer Rouge are turning Cambodian society upside down, remaking it in the image of some earlier agrarian time, casting aside everything that belongs to the old system, which has been dominated by the consumer society of the cities and towns. Some of the Khmer Rouge soldiers we talk to speak of destroying the colonial heritage and use phrases like "purification of the people" and "returning the country to the peasant."

"They haven't a humanitarian thought in their heads," says Murray Carmichael, a doctor on a Red Cross surgical team, as he describes the emptying of the hospital where he worked. "They threw everyone out—paralytics, critical cases, people on plasma. Most will die. It was just horrible."

On the second day in the embassy—April 18—the French

ask us to be ready to turn in our passports the next day so they can catalog who is in the compound. This means that what we feared is true: the Cambodians with us cannot be protected. I discuss the situation with the drivers, Hea and Sarun. They agree that their chances are better if they leave the embassy now on their own rather than later in a conspicuous group of hundreds of Cambodians. I give each of them a thousand dollars in hundred-dollar bills for potential bribe money. We have a hard time looking at each other as our parting nears. At 2:25 p.m., Hea and Sarun and their families, loaded with sacks of food and other needs, slip out a rear gate that a French guard quietly opens for them, and head north out of the city.

We have one last hope for Pran: Jon Swain happens to have a second British passport. It is in Swain's name, but we think we can doctor it and alter the name skillfully enough to give Pran a foreign identity. Al Rockoff sets to work with a pen, a razor blade and some glue, Swain has a hyphenated middle name, so by erasing "Jon" and "Swain" and the hyphen, Pran has a new name. But it's an upper-class English tongue twister— Ancketill Brewer—and Pran spends hours trying to learn how to pronounce it and make it his own. We substitute Pran's photo for Swain's, and the next day—April 19—we turn the passport in to the French with our own. A day later, the French come to Swain and tell him the ploy won't work; they say that the Khmer Rouge will spot the forgery as quickly as they did and that it could compromise the entire compound. They will kill him on the spot, the French say, and maybe us, too. They insist Pran has to leave.

I do not tell Pran right away. I want time to think about other possible subterfuges. I am also trying to get up the courage. My mind is a blank. I talk to Swain and others and we can think of no way to hide him. Finally I tell him.

I ask him if he understands—we have tried everything we can think of but we are stymied. He says yes, he understands. But it is I who do not understand, who cannot cope with this terrible thing. He saved my life and now I cannot protect him. I hate myself.

It does not ease my conscience or my feeling of responsibility that on the morning Pran and I have this talk, members of the embassy staff are moving through the compound, telling all the Cambodians they must leave. "We'd like to help you," one French official says, "but there's no way. If you stay here, there will be trouble. You're better off out there. It's a good moment to leave now because later the Khmer Rouge will come into the embassy to search."

Pran packs his essential belongings in a small bag. He destroys any piece of identification that might link him to foreigners or make him anything but a simple member of the working class. All the other Cambodian journalists in the embassy—most of them freelance photographers—do the same, although a few do not jettison their cameras. Some have families with them.

We give them all of our "private" food and cigarettes and Cambodian money. I also give Pran twenty-six hundred dollars for bribe money. At 10:15 a.m. on April 20, Pran and his group—twenty-one persons in all—gather at the embassy's front gate, their belongings in the back of a gasless Toyota wagon, which they will push up the road.

I put my arms around Pran and try to say something that will have meaning. But I am wordless and he is too.

I watch him pass through the gate and out of sight, and then I put my head against a building and start banging my fist on it.

Jon Swain comes over to comfort me. "There was nothing

you could do," he says. "Nothing you could do. It will be all right, you'll see. He'll make his way to the border and escape. You know how resourceful he is."

In the months and years to come, that scene—Pran passing through the gate—becomes a recurring nightmare for me. I will awake, thinking of elaborate stratagems I might have used to keep him safe and with me. I am a survivor who often cannot cope with surviving.

The night of Pran's departure, Jean Dyrac, vice-consul and senior official in the embassy, comes to our quarters to brief us on his latest negotiations with the Khmer Rouge. He is a decent man who had suffered cruelties as a prisoner of war during World War II. He is now overwhelmed and drained by the demands on him, by the appeals to save lives, appeals he has been powerless to respond to. He talks small talk at us first—he has made no headway with the Communists—and then his feelings begin to show. He is suffering remorse and heartache over the expulsion of the Cambodians from the compound. "We are not policemen," he says, "but we had to turn them out. They could have been shot on the spot, and those believed responsible would be compromised." His eyes well up now and his voice falters, the words coming out so painfully soft we have to strain to hear. "It is a very sad thing to say. When we do such things, we are no longer men." Unable to continue, he walks swiftly from the room, looking at no one. I feel very close to Jean Dyrac at that moment.

The next day, April 21, the rest of the Cambodians in the embassy—there are several hundred left—are forced to leave. It is a time of mass grief. Cambodian husbands are separated from European wives. Wailing rends the compound.

Louisette Praet, a Belgian woman whose Cambodian husband, an engineer, is being taken from her, is crying softly into her handkerchief. He embraces her and whispers: *"Courage, ma cherie. Courage."* But she cannot control herself, and her small body shakes with her sobs as their two little daughters look on, uncomprehending.

Vong Sarin, a Cambodian friend who had held a senior job in the former government's communications system, is turning his seven-month-old boy over to a Frenchwoman to care for. He gives me some money to put in a bank for the boy. "Do you think they will punish people like me?" he asks. I cannot tell him what I really think. "I doubt it," I say. "You were not a soldier or politician." He and I both know the truth is elsewhere, and his face remains fixed in gloom. His wife is hysterical at having to give up her child and about what awaits them. She grabs my arm and pleads: "My first baby, my only baby! We'll never see him again. Save us, save us! Get papers for us, sir. You can do it." It was a time of not being able to look into people's eyes.

Nine days later, April 30, the final evacuation of the embassy begins. The first of two truck convoys sets out at dawn for the border with Thailand, carrying about five hundred of the eight hundred foreigners in the compound. I am on it. We awake to pack at 2 a.m., and as I am leaving our building an hour later to walk to the trucks, I see in the foyer a huge vinyl suitcase that someone has discarded. It is large enough for Pran to have crawled into; I could have cut air holes in it for him. I stand frozen for a minute to breathe, looking at it, and then someone is calling me, telling me if I don't hurry, I'll miss the convoy. I move on woodenly.

Three and a half days later—after a monsoon-soaked journey whose metronome had swung crazily between petty fights among the evacuees over food and the awe and fear stirred in us by the sight of the grim Khmer Rouge work gangs, under guard, building roads and dikes with their hands—we arrived at the border. As I crossed the rickety frontier bridge, the first person to greet me was Chhay Born Lay, a Cambodian reporter for the Associated Press, who had left Phnom Penh on a press-evacuation flight on April 12, the day the American Embassy personnel pulled out. As Lay and I embraced, he asked me where Pran was. I was able to get out the words "He couldn't come" before I started crying. Lay looked at me and understood everything and cried with me.

I went to Bangkok to write my long chronicle of the fall of Phnom Penh and our captivity for *The Times*. Then I returned to Singapore and my wife and children. I was supposed to be getting a new foreign assignment, and they were packed and ready to return to the United States for our home leave. But I was not yet prepared to face "normal" life again, and I took a long time getting myself together for the trip.

It was mid-July before we arrived in the States. My wife sensed my dropout mood and decided to stay in Los Angeles, where her family lives, until I made up my mind about what I wanted to do next. After a week there, I left for New York to see my editors, stopping first in San Francisco to look after Pran's wife, Ser Moeun, and their four children. They had settled in that city, with its large Asian population, with the help of *The Times* and a refugee-relief agency it had enlisted. *The Times* and I were sharing her living expenses.

Since her evacuation from Phnom Penh in April, Ser Moeun, then thirty, had naturally been frightened and uncertain about her future; she was in a strange country and did not speak anything but Khmer. Through interpreters, I had tried to re-assure her, by telephone and letter, but without Pran she remained disoriented. I had told her, in a letter, that "it might take some time before he can reach the border," but "I know he will be out before long." This rosy optimism had been a mistake, as I was to learn when I visited her in the cramped railroad flat that was the family's first quarters.

The children were excited to see me, but Ser Moeun was distraught and trying not to show it. We were sitting beside each other on a sofa when she broke down and ran into the bathroom. It was some time before she emerged, her eyes red, a damp washcloth in her hand. I begged her to tell me what was wrong—though certainly I knew. She hesitated a long time. Finally she said, her words falling on me like a verdict: "I thought when you come you bring Pran with you." And her tears began again. I then told her the whole story of our taking refuge at the embassy and why Pran and the other Cambodians were not allowed to stay.

Over the next few days, I kept talking to Ser Moeun—to myself, really—about the need to be strong and to keep our faith alive, that his courage, intelligence, and determination would see him through. In the ensuing years, as we followed the reports of massacres and starvation brought out by es-capees, both of us wavered in that faith many times. We had nothing else to go on; Cambodia was closed to the outside world in all the normal senses—no mail, no telephone or cable system, no government an outsider could communicate with, and no possible legal entry.

I made up scenarios to help us believe: the reason Pran had not crossed into Thailand was that he had reunited with his parents and they were too elderly and infirm to make the arduous escape attempt; or that Pran was simply being cautious and ingenious, as he had always been, and would make his move to the border only when he thought the odds of success were very good. The latter turned out to be the truth.

In New York, I finally said what I knew I had to—that I

wanted a leave of absence to write a book about Cambodia. Everyone at *The Times* understood, and the answer was yes. I returned to my family in Los Angeles, feeling relieved, even buoyed at times. But I was unable to put Pran out of my mind and every time I thought of him, I was blocked and the book would not come.

Instead, I wrote letters, searching for Pran or the tiniest glimmer of news of him, to everyone I could think of. To the government of Thailand, to the American embassies in Bangkok and Singapore, to private refugee and relief agencies working in Thailand near the border with Cambodia, to the International Red Cross, to the World Health Organization, to the United Nations' refugee organization, to journalists and other friends in Southeast Asia, and to intelligence officials and other sources operating near the border who I thought might help in some special and even extralegal way.

To some, I wrote many times, even though I knew that the odds of their being able to do anything to help Pran escape were hopeless. I had fifty prints made of each of two photographs of Pran and had them distributed along the Thai border with Cambodia. This filled my days and made me feel— sometimes—that I was doing something useful. In my mind, as long as I kept up this activity, Pran would not disappear, would not die.

One relief-official contact in Thailand who joined in the search for Pran wrote back about his own frustrations and those of other Westerners who had left Cambodian friends behind. "Everyone who came out of Cambodia," he said gloomily, "has gone through a period of almost psychotic depression at what has happened."

I used the telephone as I did the mails, making call after call to official and unofficial contacts. But for long periods of time, I did not want to see anyone face to face, not even my own family. I would closet myself in my corner of the house, and, when there were no more letters to write or calls to make, I would read every page of the local newspaper or watch television.

I could not bring myself even to visit Pran's family; I couldn't endure again Ser Moeun's "I thought when you come you bring Pran with you."

So I kept in touch with her by telephone and with letters. I also wrote persistently to the relief agency assigned to the family to discuss Ser Moeun's adjustment problems. She was and is a strong woman, but her anxiety about Pran was constant, and she, too, was not sleeping well. She had frequent dreams about Pran. Some were good; most were bad. She kept remembering an incident that had occurred just before the collapse of Phnom Penh. A picture of Pran had inexplicably fallen off the wall in their living room, smashing the glass in the frame; she had cried and cried because she interpreted this to mean he would be separated from her. Every time she recalled it, she wept again.

Ser Moeun and the children—and I—were shored up by two new friends, William and Trudy Drypolcher, he a real-estate entrepreneur who had been a reconnaissance platoon leader in Vietnam and she a business executive who had volunteered for refugee work during the collapse of Vietnam and Cambodia in 1975. They had, in effect, adopted Ser Moeun and her family in every respect but the legal one, guiding them through supermarkets, through the bus system, and through the thickets of American bureaucracy. They also became surrogate parents at report-card time, when the youngest, Titonel, showed up with top marks in everything but deportment—in which the imp regularly got "U's," for "Unsatisfactory." His teachers explained that he was a fine student but never stopped chattering in class.

Ser Moeun was learning English, but it was much more difficult for her than for the children, who were doing well in special classes. She had chosen San Francisco as their home because a small community of Cambodians had already settled there, and it was a wise decision. As the gateway for Oriental immigration into America, San Francisco has over generations built up a special system of social services for resettling people like her. Her adjustment, however, was complicated by her social worker, who believed Ser Moeun should get accustomed to living in Spartan conditions and being regarded as a member of the welfare class. The Drypolchers and I tried to convince the woman that Ser Moeun's financial support was substantial and guaranteed. But nothing we said or did made a dent in her perverse attitude.

One day, Ser Moeun's landlord—a friend of the social worker's—made a pass at her and told her that if she was "nice" to him, he would forget about the rent. Ser Moeun threw him out of the apartment. The social worker's response when Ser Moeun complained was to tell her that since she was a "refugee woman" she had to expect things like that. After a couple of years of this difficult relationship, Ser Moeun gained enough confidence, both in her English and in her ability to cope on her own, to resolve the problem, and she severed all ties with the social worker.

In February 1976, ten months after the fall of Phnom Penh, our first concrete reason to hope arrived in the mail. A letter from a friend working with refugees in Thailand, Warren Hoffecker, reported that one of the refugees, a man who had gone to high school with Pran, brought out a report that Pran had been seen some months earlier in Siem Reap Province, driving an oxcart to pick up rice for people in his work camp. The man gave a lot of accurate details about Pran; I was persuaded the sighting was reliable. Siem Reap was Pran's home province, and that was where he was heading when he left the French Embassy. I told Ser Moeun the good news but also cautioned her that it might still be a long time before Pran could make his way out.

Hoffecker, in his letter, said he faced the same burden—of telling Cambodian friends that their relatives inside might not be coming out for a long time. "Try to find some gentle way of getting her to accept the fact," he wrote, adding with sardonic sadness: "There must be a less agonizing way of making a living than attempting to explain that the era of American miracles is over and there is nothing you can do."

Hoffecker had some good contacts with members of an anti-Communist resistance group, which periodically sent armed patrols into Cambodia to gather information, harass the Khmer Rouge, and sometimes to extract people. I offered a reward if they could find Pran and bring him out. Warren made the arrangements. These guerrillas continued their forays, but they never located Pran. There was only one more reported sighting of this kind. A year later, in the spring of 1977, two of my sources independently reported that Pran had been seen in Kompong Thom, a province in central Cambodia a long distance from Siem Reap. They also said the reports indicated that he had become active in some capacity in the resistance.

None of this made much sense—why would he move to the interior, away from the border? why would he suddenly take up arms now, when he had no training as a soldier?—but these sources had been reliable in the past, and I clutched at the news as at a life preserver. If he was still alive, two years after the Communist takeover, with at least hundreds of thousands of others dead by massacre and disease, then I had a chance to see him again.

When Pran escaped last October, I asked him about these reports. The first was correct: he had been driving an oxcart in Siem Reap in the latter half of 1975. The second was erroneous: he was never in Kompong Thom Province. But one of his brothers had been there, whose name was very similar— Dith Prun. When the Vietnamese army overran Cambodia early in 1979 and overthrew the Khmer Rouge, Pran finally learned what had happened to Prun, the oldest of his three brothers.

Prun had been a colonel in the Lon Nol army. He escaped to Kompong Thom with his wife and five children in 1975. For more than two years, until late 1977, he was able to conceal his military past, but then someone informed on him. The Khmer Rouge murdered the entire family. One report Pran received said that all seven were thrown alive to crocodiles.

In the spring of 1976, I returned to work at *The Times* as assistant metropolitan editor. That same week, the Pulitzer Prizes for 1975 were announced, and I won it in the foreign reporting category for my coverage of Cambodia; I accepted it on behalf of Pran and myself.

My family joined me in New York the following year. Though pieces of the book were written, it was nowhere near finished. Regardless, I felt I had to come back to the real world.

I continued to write letters and make telephone calls in my search for Pran, but my job gave me little time now to get depressed.

Ser Moeun would call, troubled, from time to time. Newspaper reports of the mass killings in Cambodia would stir her doubts again, and she would ask me to tell her once again exactly what Pran had said when he left the French Embassy. "Was he going to try for the border? What did he say about me and the children?" What she was really asking me, but was afraid to put into words, was whether I thought Pran could still be alive. And I kept saying, as much for me as for her, that I knew he would eventually emerge safe. Early in 1978, one of her woman friends in the Cambodian community suggested to Ser Moeun that she ought to think about remarrying, at least for the children's sake. The woman mentioned a well-to-do Cambodian widower who was looking for a wife. Ser Moeun dismissed the notion out of hand. She was going to wait for Pran.

The miracle began to happen shortly after 9 a.m. on April 18, 1979. I was shaving and the phone rang. It was Andreas Freund of our Paris bureau. "I have good news for you, Sydney," he said. And then he told me that an East German correspondent based in Paris had been traveling through Cambodia in a group of Soviet-bloc journalists; while in Siem Reap he had met Pran and was carrying a message from him for me. The message had eight words, in English—the eight most exquisite words I have ever heard: "Dith Pran survivor, living in Siem Reap Angkor." I wanted to kiss Andreas through the phone; someday I'll do it in person.

I then called the East German, Gerhard Leo, who works for *Neues Deutschland*. Like a crazy man, I pumped him for every last detail about Pran. He told me, with a calm that was the reverse of my excitement, that he had been approached by Pran near the temple complex of Angkor Wat on February 15. Pran took Leo aside where they could not be overheard and, in French, asked him to take the message to me. "It will make him happy," Leo quoted Pran as saying. Pran also told Leo his general background—that he had worked for *The Times*, that he had evacuated his wife and children before the Khmer Rouge came, and that he had survived under the Khmer Rouge by passing himself off as a member of the working class.

All this took place shortly after the Vietnamese army swept through Cambodia in January 1979, pushing out the Khmer Rouge government and installing their own client regime; the dozen Soviet-bloc journalists were there through the auspices of the Vietnamese and their Moscow allies. Leo apologized for the two-month delay in getting me the message but explained that, after visiting Cambodia, he had gone back to Vietnam to cover the Chinese invasion of that country and had only just returned to Paris.

He said Pran seemed to be in "relatively good health." Moreover, Pran had asked Leo to take a picture of him and send that to me, too. That photograph—of Pran in Vietcong-style black pajamas standing in front of some lesser Angkor Wat temples—has been sitting, framed, on my office desk ever since.

Having the picture of him in front of me served wishfully—but not realistically—to mute my fears. From all the refugee reports, it was clear that being alive on one day in Cambodia was no guarantee of being alive the next.

Yet despite these constantly depressing reports, neither I nor Ser Moeun—as we kept our long-distance vigil—could have conjured, or wanted to conjure, the true misery and madness of the life that had been imposed on Pran inside Cambodia.

On April 20, 1975, when Pran and his group left the French Embassy and headed to the northwest in the chaos of the forced exodus, he still held some hope that life under the Khmer Rouge would be tenable. But within a day or so, he knew differently. The Communist soldiers were treating people like livestock; they were slashing the tires on cars to force people to walk; they used ideological words he had never heard before; they seemed totally alien. By the fourth day, when he reached the river town of Prek Kdam, twenty miles out of Phnom Penh, he had decided on his plan.

He threw away his regular Western-style street clothes and put on a working-class disguise, that of a lowly taxi driver— dirty shirt, short pants, sandals, a traditional Cambodian neck- erchief. He also got a shorter haircut and threw away the twenty-six hundred dollars I had given him, since money was useless in the new Cambodia and it could only incriminate him.

"I could tell they were lying to the people to get them to cooperate," he says. "They told us we were only going to the countryside for a few days, because the Americans were going to bomb Phnom Penh."

"If you tell the truth, or argue even a little, they kill you" was Pran's simple rule of survival. "They told us all people are one class now, only working-class, peasants." So he cen- sored his thoughts and watched his vocabulary, keeping it crude and limited, to conceal his education and journalistic past. He talked as little as possible, and then softly and obsequiously. "I make myself a quiet man, like a Buddhist monk." He feigned total ignorance of politics. "I did not care if they thought I was a fool," he says. Inner discipline was a tenet of his sur- vival. "I must resist in every way until I have victory." "Resist" is a word he uses constantly in telling his story.

Not every Cambodian—or even every journalist who had worked with Westerners—was as astute as Pran. At Prek Kdam,

Pran met Sophan, a cameraman for CBS, sitting calmly by the side of the road with his two wives, four children, and sister-in-law. "Sophan was happy," Pran recalls. "When the soldiers asked him, he told them who he was and turned over his camera and film. He believed they were going to let him be a cameraman for the new government."

Wary, Pran exchanged only a few words with Sophan, told him he did not trust the Khmer Rouge, and shuffled quickly away in his new lower-class guise. Some time later, friends told Pran that Sophan and his entire family had been executed.

The first major Khmer Rouge checkpoint Pran encountered was at Phao, about forty miles out of Phnom Penh. Here the Communists were screening everyone meticulously. "They talked gently," Pran recalls. "'Tell us the truth about who you are,' they said. 'No one will be punished.' Most people believed them. They caught many big officials and military officers this way at Phao."

Pran told them his by-now polished tale of being a civilian taxi driver, and the Khmer Rouge accepted it. "They asked me where my wife and children were, and I told them that in the confusion we became separated and they were lost to me."

Pran received an identity card and moved on. Within a month, he reached the village of Dam Dek, about twenty miles east of his hometown of Siem Reap. He stopped there—and stayed for two and a half years—"because villagers told me the Khmer Rouge farther on were very brutal."

They were hardly benign in Dam Dek. Pran witnessed many beatings, with heavy staves and farm implements, and knew of many killings. "They did not kill people in front of us," he recalls. "They took them away at night and murdered them with big sticks and hoes, to save bullets." Life was totally controlled, and the Khmer Rouge did not need a good reason to kill someone; the slightest excuse would do—a boy and girl holding hands, an unauthorized break from work. "Anyone they didn't like, they would accuse of being a teacher or a student or a former Lon Nol soldier, and that was the end."

Famine set in right away in Dam Dek, as it did across the entire country. The war had disrupted all farming and the next harvest would be too little, too late. Pran believes that maybe 10 percent of the Cambodian population of more than seven million died of starvation in 1975 alone, especially older people and children.

Early on, Pran secretly bartered his gold wedding band for some extra rice—but it didn't last very long. Eventually, the rice ration in Dam Dek was reduced to one spoonful per person per day. The villagers, desperate, ate snails, snakes, insects, rats, scorpions, tree bark, leaves, flower blossoms, the trunk of banana plants; sometimes they sucked the skin of a water buffalo. Reports reached Pran's village that to the west the famine was even more severe and that some people were digging up the bodies of the newly executed and cooking the flesh.

By October 1975, Pran—then part of a work gang planting and tending the rice fields—had become so weak that he needed a wooden staff to keep himself standing. He could not raise his legs high enough to cross the knee-high embankments around the paddies, so he would lower his body onto these knolls and roll himself over. His face grew puffy with malnutrition, and his teeth began coming loose. He feared he was dying. So he took a very grave risk.

One night, during the harvest season, he slipped out of his hut of tinder wood and thatch, crawled into a nearby paddy, and began picking rice kernels and stuffing them into his pocket. Suddenly, out of the darkness, two guards rose up. Pran tried to run, but his legs gave out and he fell. He pleaded with them, saying he was only stealing a little rice because he was starving. They called a dozen members of the village committee—ten men and two women—who began beating him with long, bladed implements used for cutting bamboo. He crumpled to the ground. They continued pounding him, shouting: "You are the enemy. You were stealing rice from the collective." "I thought they were going to cut my head off," he says.

They paused in their beating only to tie his hands tightly behind his back and lead him away to a more desolate spot. "Let's kill him," the leader of the group said. But another Khmer Rouge cadre, who liked Pran because he was a good worker, urged mercy. No decision was made, and Pran, trussed and swollen and bleeding, was left kneeling in the open all night to await his fate. It began to rain. "I prayed and prayed to Buddha for my life," he says. "I said if my mother's milk had value, my life would be saved."

By morning, the man who had counseled against the death penalty had persuaded the others. Pran was paraded before the entire commune of six hundred and denounced for his "crime." He was forced to swear that he would never again break the commune's rules. The oath he was made to pronounce was "If I break the rule, I will give my life to you, to do with as you please."

Once released, he took another risk. Following Buddhist custom, he shaved his head as a sign of gratitude for his salvation. The practice of religion had been forbidden by the Khmer Rouge; all statues of Buddha had been destroyed; monks had been either killed or made to work in the fields as common laborers. Pran's act could have brought another death sentence down upon him.

Somehow, he got by again. When the Khmer Rouge asked

him why he had cut off all his hair, he told them he had been having severe headaches and thought this might help. In this land of primitive medical practices, the Communists believed him.

This behavior may seem paradoxical to us, but not to Pran. Although for four years he went to extraordinary lengths to hide his background from the Khmer Rouge in order to stay alive, he never in heart denied himself or his upbringing. He prayed silently all the time. And he never changed his name, the one obvious mark that could have given him away, should anyone have recognized him and turned him in.

"Your name is given to you by your mother and father and by Buddha," he says. "If you are a good person, your name will be lucky and Buddha will protect you."

From 1975 through late 1977, Pran remained in Dam Dek, working at a series of arduous jobs: carrying earth to build the paddy embankments, harvesting and threshing the crop, cooking for a district cooperative of eighteen blacksmiths who forged farm tools, plowing with a team of horses, cutting and sawing trees in the jungle, fishing with hand nets in the Tonle Sap Lake. The work day ran from 4 a.m. to 6 p.m. and during the harvest season, in December and January, a few extra hours at night for threshing. The Communists called these the "assault" months, because everyone had to work faster and harder.

The Draconian rules of life turned Cambodia into a nationwide gulag, as the Khmer Rouge imposed a revolution more radical and brutal than any other in modern history—a revolution that disturbed even the Chinese, the Cambodian Communists' closest allies. Attachment to home village and love of Buddha, Cambodian verities, were replaced by psychological reorientation, mass relocation, and rigid collectivization.

Families were separated, with husbands, wives, and children

all working on separate agricultural and construction projects. They were often many miles apart and did not see each other for seasons at a time. Sometimes children were separated completely from their parents, never to meet again. Work crews were sex-segregated. Those already married needed special permission, infrequently given, to meet and sleep together. Weddings were arranged by the Khmer Rouge, en masse; the pairings would simply be called out at a commune assembly. Waves of suicides were the result of these forced marriages. Children were encouraged, even trained, to spy on and report their parents for infractions of the rules. "The Khmer Rouge were very clever," Pran says. "They know that young children do not know how to lie or keep secrets as well as adults, so they always ask *them* for information." Informers, old and young, were everywhere; betrayal could be purchased for a kilo of rice.

Sometimes Khmer Rouge youths were ordered to kill their teachers or even their own parents. Some carried out these acts without apparent qualm. Others were devastated. Pran remembers a case in his district in which a man was identified as an enemy of the commune, and his son, a Khmer Rouge soldier, was told to execute him. He did so, but later, alone, he put the rifle to his own head and killed himself.

Pran says he was always most afraid of those Khmer Rouge soldiers who were between twelve and fifteen years old; they seemed to be the most completely and savagely indoctrinated. "They took them very young and taught them nothing but discipline. Just take orders, no need for a reason. Their minds have nothing inside except discipline. They do not believe any religion or tradition except Khmer Rouge orders. That's why they killed their own people, even babies, like we might kill a mosquito. I believe they did not have any feelings about human life because they were taught only discipline."

Pran interviewing a government soldier about the intensive American bombing as Schanberg takes notes, early August 1973 (the bombing ended by order of Congress on August 15). The soldier, like most members of the Cambodian army, including its highest generals, wears a scarf filled with good-luck amulets.

Schanberg crossing the Mekong with government troops and civilians to get to Neak Luong, 1973. (*Sarah Webb Barrell*)

Left: Keo Chan, a government soldier, weeps for his wife and ten of his eleven children, killed in Neak Luong during an accidental American bombing on August 6, 1973, while he was on sentry duty a few miles away. (*Sydney H. Schanberg*)

Below, left: Schanberg watching a folk play performed on a flatbed truck in the heart of the city during a Buddhist religious holiday, October 1973. (*Sarah Webb Barrell*)

Opposite: Man with child at Oudong, twenty miles northwest of Phnom Penh, before a gilt Buddha in the historic temple there, heavily damaged during the war, July 1974. (*Sydney H. Schanberg*)

Opposite, inset: A boy soldier in the government army—many children joined up, and lied about their ages—in November 1974. (*Sydney H. Schanberg*)

A soldier's wife holds plasma for her husband while they await helicopter evacuation from Neak Luong, under heavy bombardment and surrounded by the Khmer Rouge, early 1975. (*Sydney H. Schanberg*)

At the city limits of Phnom Penh, a woman with her pig and other belongings flees the advancing Khmer Rouge and its rockets and mortar attacks; a rubber-sandal factory burns in the background. (*Sydney H. Schanberg*)

Acting Ambassador Thomas Enders greets Prime Minister Long Boret at an official ceremony.

Children watch the evacuation of Americans from Phnom Penh at the Marines' improvised helicopter pad, April 12, 1975. (*Dith Pran*)

Ambassador John Gunther Dean, in a dark suit and carrying the American Embassy flag, with Deputy Chief of Mission Robert Keeley behind him, and with bodyguards and Marines, leaving Phnom Penh in the helicopter evacuation, April 12, 1975. (*Ennio Iacobucci*)

As the Khmer Rouge break through the capital's final defenses, villagers and country people flood to the Red Cross's "protected international zone" at the Hotel Le Phnom; they were taken in and sheltered there after being disarmed, April 16, 1975. (*Ennio Iacobucci*)

A jeep loaded with civilians, including monks, one of them seated on the windshield waving a white flag of surrender, moves down a Phnom Penh street to welcome Khmer Rouge troops, April 17, 1975. (*Ennio Iacobucci*)

Pran talking to a smiling Khmer Rouge soldier—the only cordial encounter he or Schanberg had with the Khmer Rouge—in front of the post office, April 17, 1975. (*Sydney H. Schanberg*)

A Khmer Rouge soldier in Phnom Penh, in front of the Ministry of Information, April 17, 1975. (*Sydney H. Schanberg*)

Opposite, above: French-Cambodian mixed families living on the grounds of the French Embassy after April 17, 1975. (*Ennio Iacobucci*)

Opposite, below: Western journalists and relief officials listen to BBC World Service radio news at the French Embassy after April 17, 1975. (*Ennio Iacobucci*)

Schanberg and other journalists who had witnessed the surrender of Phnom Penh to the Khmer Rouge cross into Thailand; Sylvain Julienne, a French freelance photographer, carries his adopted Cambodian daughter, May 3, 1975. (*AP Radio*)

Opposite: Detail of mass grave at Cheung Ek, in Kandal Province, where more than 8,000 bodies were discovered, 1981. (*David Hawk*)

The two photographs of Pran that Schanberg circulated by the dozen to relief officials along the Thai-Cambodian border and in refugee camps: (*left*) Pran wearing a *krama*, the traditional Cambodian scarf, at Kompong

Som, a tourist center and Cambodia's only deep-water port, late 1973
(*Sarah Webb Barrell*); (*right*) a portrait photo taken at the My Ho photo
shop in Phnom Penh, 1974.

Im Prem, Pran's paternal uncle (*left*), and Dith Proeung, his father (*right*), in front of his parents' house in Siem Reap, early 1974.

Lieutenant Colonel Dith Prun, Pran's oldest brother, early 1975.

Opposite: Meak Ep, Pran's mother, sixty-seven, on the verandah of the family home in Siem Reap, early 1984.

Pran and Schanberg as they leave the Surin refugee camp, where they had been reunited the day before, October 10, 1979.

Pran reunited with his family in San Francisco, October 19, 1979.

Pran and his family in Brooklyn, December 1984: (*left to right*) Pran, Ser Moeun, Titonel, Titonath, Hemkary, and Titony.

Pran and Schanberg, January 8, 1985.
(*John McDonnell, The Washington Post*)

Louis Schanberg with his son and Pran at the premiere of
The Killing Fields, October 30, 1984.

Outsiders have asked, in the years since 1975, how a people known as the "smiling, gentle Khmers" could have produced such a holocaust. The image of a bucolic, carefree people was, of course, simplistic—an illusion that foreigners preferred to see. All cultures are complex and all have their hidden savage sides waiting to erupt. The Nazi horror in World War II and the 1947 partition of India in which Hindus and Moslems slaughtered each other by the thousands are but two vivid examples. Nonetheless, the Khmer Rouge terror may have touched a level of cruelty not seen before in our lifetime. It was Cambodians endlessly killing other Cambodians.

Even the victims could not fathom whence the Khmer Rouge had come or how they had been created. "I look at them and do not know them," Pran says. "To me, they are not Khmers."

With their cruelty, the Khmer Rouge brought a new language—words with a dehumanized ring, a mechanical robot-like quality, euphemisms for atrocity, words that people had never heard before. There was the omnipresent *Angka*—the word for the Khmer Rouge regime itself. It means simply "the organization." No explanations were ever given for policy, just "*Angka* says" or "*Angka* orders." People were called *opakar*, or "instruments." The Khmer nation was called "machine," from the French or English—strange for a government trying to erase the colonial past.

And then there was a sinister word, a word with a deceptively polite sound, *sneur*, which means "invite" or "ask." The Khmer Rouge would come to someone's house, Pran explains, and *sneur* someone's son to study or to be educated. Lulled by the gentleness of the request, many went without a protest. But people quickly realized that those who had been *sneured* never came back; the word took on a new meaning: "take away and kill."

Fear and suspicion became the essence of existence. To trust

anyone was to risk one's life. People stopped having mean-
ingful conversations, even secretly, even inside their own family. (In July 1979, when Pran decided to make his escape
attempt, he was too fearful to tell his mother or sister, who
were the only survivors in his family. He was not afraid they
would inform on him, but maybe the conversation would be
overheard. Or maybe his family would say something inad-
vertently that would spell trouble for him. "You get used to
keeping secrets," he says. "You decide it's better not to tell
anything to anybody. I was afraid. Maybe my mother tries to
talk me out of it. She worries, she loves me, I am her only
son left. What if someone hears her talking?")

In the spring of 1977, a group of "moderates" in the Khmer
Rouge leadership plotted a coup. They were discovered by the
ruling group and wiped out. But *Angka* did not stop there.
Fresh troops were sent to every district to replace and sometimes execute "untrustworthy" ones. The search was intensified
for people like Pran, educated people from the Western-oriented
past. The cold and wooden teenaged troops did not need evidence; their slaughter was wholesale—teachers, village chiefs,
students, sometimes whole villages.

In late 1977, Pran made a move to another village, spurred
by these fresh upheavals throughout the country, a new wave
of purges and killings, and disquietude on his part that some
fanatic villagers in Dam Dek were growing suspicious of him.
"There were more killings in 1977 than in 1975," Pran says.
"I saw many arrested in my village, hands tied behind their
backs, crying for their lives. I got chills down my back, like
fever. I kept on talking softly, pretending to support *Angka*. I
prayed every day and every night, in my mind." As the radical
fervor grew in Dam Dek, Pran looked for a way out.

During 1976 and 1977, he had become acquainted with the

commune chief and others in the village of Bat Dangkor, four miles to the north. They seemed to him "not so pro-Communist and more compatible."

Movement from place to place was rigidly controlled and rarely allowed by the Khmer Rouge, but somehow, through gentle pleading and by playing the empty-headed worker, he got permission to move.

Life immediately improved for Pran. Though his work regimen remained severe and food was still not plentiful, his commune chief, a twenty-seven-year-old named Phat who had lost his love for the Khmer Rouge, took a liking to him. Pran became his houseboy, carrying water, chopping firewood, bathing the children, building the fire, washing clothes, and cooking. The days were long, but Pran felt somewhat protected. "I did everything to please him," Pran says. "I was like a slave."

This commune chief had a radio, and sometimes at night— maybe once a week—Pran and four or five trusted friends would gather around it with him and surreptitiously listen to the Voice of America. The V.O.A. came on at 8:30 p.m., and it was on these broadcasts that Pran learned of the fierce fighting throughout 1978 between the Khmer Rouge and the Vietnamese army along the border with Vietnam.

Though both governments were Communist, the Cambodians and Vietnamese were centuries-old ethnic enemies, and now the Chinese were supporting the Khmer Rouge and the Russians were supporting the Vietnamese. Vietnam, in its propaganda broadcasts, called Cambodia "a land of blood and tears, hell on earth," and announced the formation of a new "front" to "liberate" Cambodia. Pran took some hope from this; anything was better than the insane Khmer Rouge.

Finally, in December, he learned on the V.O.A. that the

Vietnamese had invaded Cambodia in force. On January 7, 1979, they took Phnom Penh. Three days later, they reached the Siem Reap area, and the Khmer Rouge units around Pran's village took flight.

After about a week of careful watching, Pran was persuaded that the Vietnamese were not killing civilians and were allowing people to return to their home villages. So, his spirits up but still cautious, he left Bat Dangkor by moonlight and, smiling a lot at his "liberators" on the way, he walked the twenty-odd miles to the town of Siem Reap to search for his family.

What he found was what most Cambodians found when they returned home: a few survivors but most of their family members dead. Of his mother and father, three brothers, two sisters, and numerous nephews and nieces, only his sixty-three-year-old mother, one sister, a sister-in-law, and five nieces and nephews were alive. One brother, nineteen, had been executed for being a student, the other two for being military officers in the Lon Nol army. One sister had been killed for being the wife of an officer. The sister who survived still had three children; a fourth child was lost to starvation.

Pran's father, a retired public-works official, had died of starvation in late 1975, about the same time that Pran was caught and beaten for stealing the pocketful of rice in Dam Dek. As he lay dying, he called out for Pran's wife, Ser Moeun, who had been close to him and had often brought him special treats from her kitchen. "Ser Moeun, Ser Moeun," he rambled deliriously as his life slipped away, "bring me some of your food and cake."

As Pran re-explored Siem Reap, people kept walking up to him in astonishment, saying, "I thought you died. How did you stay alive?" "Because of my education and background," he says, "no one could believe I could survive."

The reasons for their disbelief lay all around Siem Reap; they were called the "killing fields." "One day soon after I came back," Pran recalls, "two women from my village went looking for firewood in the forest. They found bones and skulls everywhere among the trees and in the wells. When they came back they told me about it and said they would take me there and show me. They asked me, 'Are you afraid of ghosts?' I told them, 'No, why should I be afraid? The ghosts may be my brothers or my sister.'"

So Pran went to see the killing fields. Each of the two main execution areas alone, he says, held the bones of four to five thousand bodies, thinly covered by a layer of earth.

"In the water wells, the bodies were like soup bones in broth," he says. "And you could always tell the killing grounds because the grass grew taller and greener where the bodies were buried."

Similar reports have come from every village in Cambodia: tall green grass and choked wells.

The Vietnamese "liberators," having seized the main towns, set up a client Cambodian government in Phnom Penh and were looking for administrators to help them govern throughout the country. In Siem Reap, local villagers who knew Pran's skills asked for him as their administrative chief, and the two Vietnamese governors of the province agreed. He became, in effect, the mayor of Siem Reap township, which held about ten thousand people. "I took the job out of pity for my people," he says. "They wanted a Cambodian in charge, so I take it to lift them up. There were so few intellectuals still alive. If I don't do it, who will lead and help my people?"

In his new job, Pran wore a khaki uniform with a Soviet-style military cap and carried an AK-47 automatic rifle. Every week he had to give a speech, cleared first by the Vietnamese, to a different section of the population in his township. "I don't talk politics," he says. "I just talk about nationalism, about how you have to work for food. I urge people to work because of the starvation and the low economy."

The two Vietnamese governors, Nhien and Linh, praised him often and showed him considerable respect, "because I helped them a lot to set up the administration. Sometimes they even embraced me." But Pran never stopped thinking about escape. It was during this period that he had cautiously approached the East German correspondent Gerhard Leo and asked him to carry that message—"Dith Pran survivor"—to me. The Vietnamese governors had directed Pran to arrange a welcoming committee of fifty villagers for the journalists, which is how Pran came to be there.

While cheered somewhat by the arrival of the foreigners, he was reluctant at first to approach the group, out of fear that giving away his *New York Times* background might put him in jeopardy. But then he saw Leo walking away from the main group to take some pictures and heard him speaking in French mixed with English. "I was afraid by now of all Communists," he said, "but when he was alone I decided to take a risk because he's a long-nose [Westerner]."

Five months later, Pran's fears were realized. His Vietnamese superiors somehow discovered, perhaps through an informer, that he had worked for American journalists. They called him in, told him he was politically "unclean," said his mind was tainted by "unrevolutionary thoughts," and forced him to resign his job. On July 15, 1979, an election was held in Siem Reap to fill Pran's post. He grew increasingly nervous about what the Vietnamese might do to him now that they had found him out.

The news about Pran from Gerhard Leo in April 1979 put me in a state of euphoria, but it also made me desperate. I knew he had been safe on February 15, but I had no clue as to what was happening to him now. So I began exploring every possible way to get further news of him, to get a message to him, to get him out of the country. Through friends, I quietly sounded out the Vietnamese, but they were unwilling to help, saying it was a domestic Cambodian matter.

I renewed my contacts with international agencies, some of whom were just then making efforts to open relief programs inside Cambodia. The next several months were marked by many long-distance telephone calls, cables in coded language, the passing of money to my contacts in the event bribes were necessary on Pran's behalf once they got inside Cambodia, and, throughout, the private help of Henry Kamm, *The Times*'s correspondent in Bangkok, whose dedicated and gifted re-porting—perhaps more than any other factor—had made the world aware of the enormity of the refugee problem in Indo-china.

In July, my contacts, who were now in Phnom Penh but who could not get to the Siem Reap area, reported that third parties had seen Pran again there on May 7. A later report, in August, said he was okay in the latter part of July, working in some vague capacity for the Vietnamese-installed province committee. Also in August, my contacts sent a cautiously worded letter to Pran through a third party who was going to Siem Reap. It said that I had received his message of survival from Gerhard Leo, that I and his family were "anxious" about "your health," and that if possible he should send either a verbal or written reply back to my contacts in Phnom Penh. My sources were convinced that Pran received this letter—which would have been the first confirmation to him since April 1975 that I had been searching for him and now knew he was alive. But no reply came back from him as I waited nervously through August and September; my contacts were due to come out of Cambodia in early October, and I kept reassuring myself that they would be carrying direct news from Pran.

Pran never did get that letter. In fact, until our reunion on October 9, I was never able to get word to him that his message had reached me or to give him any sign at all of my long search for him. We were functioning in two different worlds, each darkened to the other. While I was counting on his remaining safe and fixed in Siem Reap as I maneuvered through my contacts to extract him from the country through official channels, he took the step he had been planning and dreaming of for four and a half years — he made his move for the border.

On July 29, his relationship with the Vietnamese having broken down, he slipped quietly out of Siem Reap for the village of Phum Trom, forty miles to the northwest. He headed for Phum Trom because he had heard that the anti-Communist resistance, known as *Sereika* ("liberation"), was active there and was helping people to escape. After six weeks of preparation in that village, he and eleven other men set out before dawn on a morning in mid-September.

In a straight line, the border with Thailand to the north was only about thirty-five miles away. But their route was as the snake crawls — sixty miles — weaving and turning and climbing across brambled jungle and rocky hills to avoid roving bands of Khmer Rouge guerrillas, Vietnamese patrols, deadly punji traps (sharpened bamboo stakes smeared with toxic matter and covered with leaves and brush) and unmarked mine fields.

At noon on the second day of their exodus, they stopped briefly to rest. When they rose to start again, Pran, who had been toward the end of the single file, by happenstance began walking third in line. A few minutes later, the two men in front of him, only fifteen feet ahead, were dead; they had stepped on a mine. A piece of shrapnel hit Pran in the left side, but it was only a flesh wound and he was able to run on with the others.

They reached the border on the fourth day. Pran's companions had clandestine contacts there; he did not. So, afraid of being arrested by Thai authorities if he crossed over, he waited for seventeen days just a few hundred yards on the Cambodian side—in a no-man's-land where he was reasonably safe—watching for the right moment to get across and into the sanctuary of a Cambodian refugee camp fifteen miles away. (During this frustrating wait, he sent letters to me through a courier, who was supposed to mail them from the nearby town of Prasat. Only one ever reached me, and it arrived long after our reunion.)

On the seventeenth day—October 3—with the help of friends who provided him with a uniform worn by the Cambodian resistance, which satisfied the Thais, he crossed the frontier and made it to the refugee camp.

Although finally free, he was still insecure because he was an "illegal"—an unregistered refugee—and could technically be pushed back into Cambodia (the Thais had done this to several thousand Cambodians some months before). Pran instantly searched out an American relief official in the camp, Ruth Ellison, told her his history, and asked her to get word to me through the American Embassy or *The Times*'s correspondent in Bangkok. Miss Ellison, who, with her mother and father, had been working in the camp for years, representing a missionary group, called an embassy official as soon as she reached her home in Surin that night. He called Henry Kamm, who called my office. It was Thursday morning, October 4. I was not in yet, and he left no message except that I should call him. My attempts to reach him through the day were unsuccessful, and I was jumpy and tense all day, one moment conjuring up my wildest hope, that Pran had escaped, and the next moment trying to curb my excitement and ease the letdown should the news be innocuous or worse.

At 7:50 p.m., I try to phone Henry again. I get him this time and he says quickly: "Pran is out. He's in Thailand, in the refugee camp at Surin." Skyrockets go off in my head. I can hear Henry saying something about what he is doing at the American Embassy to speed up Pran's entry into the United States, but then I can't grasp it. I'm crying at my desk, and it doesn't matter.

I call Ser Moeun as soon as the Bangkok call is over. It is only 5 p.m. in San Francisco and she is not home yet from her job as clerk in a bank. I get the eldest son, Titony, and blurt out the news. "Hey!" he shouts, as American as a fifty-yard touchdown pass, "aaaaaaaaaallll riiiiight!" Then he turns to his sister and two brothers: "Hey, you guys! Our dad is out of Cambodia! Our dad is out of Cambodia!" They cheer and yell and bang on something. Then I call the Drypolchers and my wife. A few hours later, I get Ser Moeun. The telephone holds a lot of happiness that night.

The next few days are like a dream. I leave on the first available plane for Bangkok to get to Pran. I am high on the miracle but still full of anxiety about getting him across the last bureaucratic barriers, into this country. My plane is three hours late taking off, and it looks as if I have no chance to make my connecting flight in Athens, but that plane is very late, too, and I get on it just in time. I start believing in omens and symbols, for everything is going my way. As I enter my Bangkok hotel room on Sunday afternoon, October 7, the first thing my eyes light on is a magazine called *Business in Thailand* lying on an end table. On the cover, its lead article is billboarded in large bold type: PRAWN ON THE WAY.

There is more good fortune at the American Embassy's refugee office, where Pran's case has been given priority and the staff is being spectacularly helpful. By midday Monday, Pran has been put on a special list that will get him out of the refugee camp on Wednesday and down to Bangkok for final processing. With that done, I can leave for the border area, three hundred miles and six hours to the northeast. But without Thai government papers authorizing me to visit the camp, I shall have to wait until the next morning, Tuesday, when the relief worker, Ruth Ellison, can take me in "unofficially" with her. I go to bed in a run-down hotel in Surin shortly after midnight, but I cannot sleep. Finally I give up the attempt and rise at 4 a.m.

On the twenty-mile drive south to the camp, I make small talk to hide my nerves. At 8:40 a.m., we pass through the camp gates, and in five minutes we are outside the hut where Pran is staying with another family. I jump out and run inside, sputtering in French as I ask where Pran is. He's in the long house on stilts fifty feet away, and a young man runs to get him, shouting in Khmer: "Brother, brother, someone's here. You have a chance now. You have a chance." Then Pran comes running out of the long house—I remember in that fraction of a second thinking how hurt and vulnerable he looked—and literally leaps into my arms, his legs wrapped around my waist, his head buried in my shoulder. "You came, Syd, oh, Syd, you came." The words come sobbing out with the tears. We stand like that for several minutes until his thin frame stops shaking and his legs slip to the ground.

He looks at me then and says: "I am reborn. This is my second life."

Arms around each other's shoulders, we walk slowly into the hut and begin talking nonstop, ricocheting from one subject to another in chaotic sequences, as we grope for the meaning of our lost four and a half years.

We talk of his wife and children, of how he disguised his identity to survive the savagery of the Khmer Rouge, of old Western journalist friends, of old Cambodian friends who are now dead, of the members of his family inside Cambodia who were executed, of the Seiko digital watch he has just bought from another refugee in the camp, of the time in 1975 when he was almost beaten to death for stealing a pocketful of rice, and of the letter he wrote to me only two days before, still unaware that I had received any of the messages from him. (That letter arrives at *The Times* on October 24, a week after Pran and I reached the United States. It says in part: "Need see Schanberg. At least a cable from him. We have many things to write.") Restless, pent-up, we walk through the barren camp, sipping an orange soda, holding hands, looking long at each other. There is much waiting to be said.

With trepidation, I ask the question that has been churning inside me since that distant April in 1975. "Can you forgive me for not being able to keep you safe in the French Embassy, for leaving Cambodia without you?"

"No, no," he says, gripping my hand hard. "It's not like that. Nothing to forgive. We both made a decision. We both agree to stay, no one pushed the other. You tried all you could to keep me, but it didn't work. Not your fault. We stayed because we did not believe in a blood bath. We were fools;

we believed there would be reconciliation. But who could have believed the Khmer Rouge would be so brutal?

"We both made mistakes, both of us," he goes on, in a torrent of words that has been locked up so long. "Maybe we should have tried to buy a French passport. We had a lot of money. But I was never angry at you, even when the Khmer Rouge beat me near to death. I always missed you; sometimes I cry in the forest, thinking of you."

Why did Pran wait so long to try to escape? "My brain was always thinking how to get out," he says, "but Khmer Rouge patrols were everywhere and they had mine fields all along the border and traps made of punji sticks. I must build relations in each place where I live. I must take care with each step, to make sure I have good information and at least fifty-fifty chance of not getting killed. One time I was going to try for it but then I heard the Thais were pushing refugees back into Cambodia so I stopped the idea." When he talks about life under the Khmer Rouge, he uses phrases very unlike him— "true hell," "more than insane," "below zero."

The camp loudspeaker suddenly calls his name, summoning him to the camp office. He ignores it. I tell him that probably the embassy document has arrived, clearing him for departure to Bangkok on the following day. It has, but he is uneasy and tells me a friend of his will check it out instead. In his viscera, he is still not convinced he is free. Maybe the Thais, he thinks, will yet force him back into Cambodia. (Even when we reach Bangkok and meet old friends around the hotel pool, Pran's eyes narrow and his voice fades to a whisper whenever he talks about the Khmer Rouge and their policies. "There's no one here," I say. "You can relax." He laughs self-consciously, but he is not persuaded and looks around to see if anyone is listening.)

We start talking again about our separate thoughts and dreams since 1975. They are not very separate. Pran tells me: "I think of you all the time inside Cambodia. I imagine that you adopt one of my sons—probably Titony, the eldest—because you have only girls."

Then he adds, in a rush of memory: "Every month, under the Khmer Rouge, I have dream that you come to get me in a helicopter. I have a radio on the ground and you radio me your position." I tell him I repeatedly had the same fantasy, like a waking dream.

It all seems uncanny and it makes us both elated and yet discomposed. We laugh to break the spell and bring us back to the gritty dust of the camp. Now, more than ever before, we have lionized each other, given each other heroic dimensions. It is mystical, but it is also unreal, and we know that in the times to come we will have to deal with our respective warts and flaws and humanness.

But not just yet. He tells me he always knew I would be loyal to him and to my promises. "In Cambodia, I tell myself," he says, "if I die, I die with my eyes well closed, because I know you will always take care of my family. I trust you one hundred percent."

I tell him I prayed for him often. "Ohhh. Ohhh," he says, marveling. "That explains it. That's why I was so lucky."

I have with me the many joyous written messages from Pran's friends on *The Times*. Some of the writers had met him only through my constant tales. I now take these messages from my briefcase—the same briefcase that still carries that scruffy silk rose I squeezed for luck on the day we were captured in April 1975—and give them to Pran. As he reads, his eyes turn moist again.

Abe Rosenthal, *The Times*'s executive director, writes that "all these years...you have been in the minds of all *Times* men and women" and that the news of his return to freedom had brought "rejoicing throughout the paper."

Jim Clarity, whom Pran had shepherded to many scary battle sites, says: "Pran, you are a true hero. I am proud to know you. Now that you are safe, thanks again for keeping me safe."

Al Siegal, whom Pran also guided on a trip to Phnom Penh, writes: "With all my heart and all my love...you have given all of us another reason—the most wonderful of reasons—to be proud of our paper and our profession. We embrace you, Pran."

Joe Lelyveld, another of Pran's flock: "I feel freer today because you are free....I pray that the rest of your days will be filled with peace."

And so many more.

As Pran folds the last of the notes and puts it away, he murmurs: "They were all thinking of me. Oh, how wonderful."

Pran's mood goes up and down wildly that first day; he weeps at some unspeakable memory and then bursts into laughter over the wonder of our reunion and the good news I bring him about his family thriving in San Francisco. Yet he is concerned about how Westernized they may have become and how he will adjust to them, and they to him, after all this time. "Do they still speak Khmer?" he asks. I tell him I think they speak it often at home.

Suddenly, Pran asks me: "What about your book? Did you finish it?"

"How did you know I was writing a book?" I reply, taken aback.

"Oh," he says, "I was sure with all the notes you take and papers you save you must be going to write a book." I tell him I had become stymied on the project for many reasons, and he looks upset. But then I tell him of the Pulitzer I won and that I accepted it on his behalf as well as mine, and his face becomes incandescent.

He starts talking ebulliently and zanily about going back to work right away with me. "Can I get an American passport?" he asks. "There are many stories to do here. We could work along the border. My people are in trouble. If I had a camera, I could take pictures, too—like the old days." I remind him, laughing, that first he has to get to San Francisco just to get his American refugee-status papers and to rejoin his family, and that I have a family and job in New York. "You're crazy," I say warmly. He remains a driven reporter.

He chortles, too. "Yes, sure, I'm crazy," he says. "I still want to work as a journalist."

We also discuss the medical care he will need. His legs and feet are scarred from his march out of Cambodia. Many of his teeth are loose and rotting from malnutrition; there is a large gap between his two front teeth where porcelain fillings fell out in 1976. He keeps his hands in his pockets much of the time because when he holds them out, they shake like those of a palsied old man—also from malnutrition.

On the drive back to Bangkok the next day—October 10— we stop for breakfast at a hotel in Korat. Pran orders only milk and coffee, saying his stomach is not ready for a big meal. He is uncomfortable in the modern dining room. When he has to go to the toilet, he asks me to take him. "I feel like a monkey," he says, embarrassed.

We arrive in our hotel room in Bangkok at 2 p.m. At exactly 2:03, the message button on the telephone lights up. The post office has just delivered a large envelope from Pran's wife. In it are letters from his family and the first pictures of them he has seen since their evacuation from Phnom Penh on April 12, 1975. He opens the packet, reads the letters with tears in his eyes, and then examines the color photographs incredulously. Titonel, the youngest, was only three when they parted. Titony, now fifteen, has grown bigger and taller than his father from his rich American diet. Pran scans the pictures again and again, holds them at arm's length, and shakes his head: "I don't think I would know them if I saw them on the street," he says, in wonder. "I am sure I would not know Titonel."

Pran's first telephone call to his family is both jubilant and uneasy. The electronic reunions that occupy the first part of the call are ecstatic. But then Pran tries speaking in Khmer to the children and comes away a little distressed when he realizes that the two youngest, Titonel and Titonath, understand almost nothing of what he has said. The traditionalist father in him is troubled.

But there is something more important on his mind. He gets Ser Moeun back on the phone and tells her of the fortune-teller in Cambodia who, in early 1979, read Pran's "numbers" and told him that the forecast for his eldest son was zero— which means death or the threat of death. Pran has been worried about Titony ever since, and he now tells Ser Moeun to take him immediately to a Buddhist priest, get some holy water, and have Titony drink it. She agrees and has it done before we get to the States.

Culture shock is too mild a phrase to describe what overtook Pran in Bangkok. This was his first trip outside his own country, and Bangkok is a much more modern city than once-graceful and somnolent Phnom Penh. During his ten days in the Thai capital Pran did many things he had not been able to do for four and a half years, such as sleep in a real bed, eat a full meal (his first entree was escalopes de veau cordon bleu), wear a shirt tucked inside his pants, and use a mirror in which he could see his whole body. But other phenomena he was experiencing for the first time in his life: a department store (where he bought Wrangler corduroy jeans), a divided highway, pancakes and syrup.

Other things were traumatically new, too. When my story about his escape appeared on the front page of *The Times* on October 12, calls and cables began streaming in. Some were from elated old friends. Others were from people who wanted him to go on lecture tours, write a book, make a movie, appear on television, give interviews for magazines and newspapers.

From total disguise and anonymity and silence behind Cambodia's bamboo curtain, Pran had stepped into the blaring media age. But what possibly overwhelmed him most was the realization—from the correspondence and clippings and letters I had brought him and from the fresh communications arriving at the hotel—of how many people had been aware of him and his plight and of how many people had cared about him through his four and a half years of misery. Though baffled by it all, he was warmed by the celebrity attention. He asked me to handle all the inquiries, and I became his press secretary. Our roles were changing, and I was somewhat disoriented by it. In fact, I wasn't sure I liked it.

Among the cables was one from Jon Swain, the British journalist whose life Pran had saved along with mine when we were captured by the Khmer Rouge. It read: "Sydney, this is the most wonderful, wonderful news. Please give Pran my love and a big hug from someone who owes him everything." Pran's reply to Jon read something like a Cambodian proverb. "Hi, Jon. The world is round. Now I meet you again. Pran was in bad shape, but the life is remained. Love, Pran."

After a few days, I noticed that Pran had begun to hum and even sing again, pleasures that were not allowed in Cambodia. He was coming alive. His health, however, remained fragile.

As we pushed through the many days of medical exams, security checks, and governmental procedures—both Thai and American—necessary for final clearance to leave for San Francisco, Pran was hit by periodic waves of high fever. We both eventually suspected it might be malaria, but, afraid that detection in Thailand could lead to a long period in quarantine for Pran, we decided to treat it through the easygoing hotel doctor and with store-bought antibiotics.

The first time it happened—the night of October 12—we thought it was some kind of flu or viral infection. We didn't have a thermometer, but his body was burning up, so I threw a pile of ice cubes into a tub and made him take a cold bath. It brought the fever down somewhat, but he ached all over, so I got him back into bed, put a cold cloth on his sweating forehead, and gave him a back and head massage. I also gave him fruit juices and antibiotic tablets.

By morning, the fever had broken, and we sat around joking about the "countercolonial movement" developing in our hotel room. "*You* used to see to *my* needs," I told him, as he laughed. "Now things are reversed. What's going on?" I was getting rid of some of my pique over our changed roles; it was a healthy development.

Later, on another night when I was feeling achy and he was massaging *my* back, he told me that he had, on occasion, been ordered to give massages to Khmer Rouge troops when they were sick. "Just think of me as the Khmer Rouge," I said, continuing our jesting.

In between his fever bouts and forays into bureaucratic red tape, Pran spent his time resting, eating, and giving interviews to television and print journalists. He also kept pulling out the pictures of his children and staring at them for long periods of time.

Though he was groping with his radically changing life and

moving into the future, the past was never too far away. One morning, during a break in an interview with Australian television on the hotel's broad lawn, he saw a line of red ants marching up the trunk of a coconut palm. "That's what we used to eat for food when we had nothing else," he said in a monotone. On another morning, I felt like a swim in the pool and asked Pran to join me. "No," he said with a grimace. "I was out in the sun for four years in the rice paddies. I don't need any more."

In the middle of one night, we were startled awake by the phone. It was Sylvain Julienne, a French freelance photographer who had taken in an orphaned Cambodian infant in the days before Phnom Penh's fall and had been with us in the French Embassy. He was overjoyed by Pran's escape, but there was a shadow in his mind as well. He was desperate for news of Sou Vichith, a Cambodian photographer he was very close to. He asked Pran nervously if he knew anything about Vichith. Pran told him ruefully that the reports he heard were that Vichith died of some illness in Kompong Cham Province in the early days of Khmer Rouge control.

Our flight home to San Francisco on October 19 was an anxious eighteen-hour journey—anticipation and agitation in equal doses, as the family reunion neared. On the last leg of the flight, I turned to Pran and asked him, just out of curiosity, what was the first thing he wanted to do when he saw his family. His face spread into an elfin grin and then he just buried his head in my right shoulder and giggled and giggled in embarrassment. I told him that I had asked the question innocently, not thinking at all about marital pleasures, but he just kept giggling.

A few hours from San Francisco, the fever struck again. He popped another handful of the hotel doctor's pills into his mouth, and his temperature subsided. As we neared the shores of the United States, he became very nervous, his right knee jiggling up and down like a telegraph key gone wild.

The reunion at the airport was sweet trauma—a crush of flowers, deep hugs, tears and television cameras. After that day, Pran would have no difficulty recognizing his children on the street.

We departed for Ser Moeun's modest attached house in the Sunset section, near the ocean, where Pran's first American meal awaited. It was Kentucky Fried Chicken; Ser Moeun had been too excited to cook. The television set was turned on to a puppet show. The family album, holding all the photographs of the years he had been away, was brought to him. He could not absorb it all, and I left with the Drypolchers for their house, so that the family could be alone.

During the night, Pran's fever flared anew. Ser Moeun called us at 1:45 to say that his temperature had risen to 105 degrees. We rushed over and took him to the emergency room of Kaiser Permanente hospital. I stayed with him all night, as blood, urine, and sputum tests were made. He couldn't sleep. His mind—as it had repeatedly since our reunion—raced over the past and he chattered in a stream of consciousness about our adventures in the good old days.

About the day our car broke down past the airport in desolate emptiness—almost into Khmer Rouge territory—and we frantically tried to push it back toward Phnom Penh and finally got a push from a government truck whose driver was as nervous as we were. And about the day the Khmer Rouge seized Phnom Penh and trained their rockets on the Hotel Le Phnom and ordered all the Westerners out and we took pictures of them with their rockets and Pran joked about getting the pictures developed at our regular photo shop, My Ho, and mailing them to the Khmer Rouge. And on and on he went.

By midmorning, his illness was definitely diagnosed as malaria. Prescriptions were written for chloroquine and prima-quine, and we took him home.

Later he told me: "When we were in the hospital that night, you were exhausted, but still you take care of me. I look at your face and I think, you and I, it seems like we are born from the same mother. I kept talking about everything else," he explained, "because it was very difficult to tell you these things."

A few days later it is time for another difficult parting, for I must return to New York, while he recovers his health.

Even though the leave-taking is only temporary, it is dis-quieting nonetheless for both of us. It is my turn now to manufacture diverting conversation, choosing a tone of avun-cular guidance, as I tell him to follow the doctor's orders, open a checking account, take long walks, eat well, et cetera.

Then, in a futile attempt to hide my feelings and lighten the moment, I tease him about our old argument in Phnom Penh on that day when I pushed him hard to tell me "the whole truth," an argument that had since become a kind of special folklore between us. That argument had ended with Pran saying he could not tell me the entire truth, only eighty percent of it, because "twenty percent I have to keep for myself."

"Is it still only eighty percent?" I ask now, gibing at him fondly.

"No, not anymore," he says, in a tone as solemn as mine was airy. "There is nothing to hide. No more secrets. No more camouflage. We both have the same blood."

EPILOGUE

As I write this postscript, it is more than five years since Pran escaped and I wrote the original story. The people of Cambodia still live in a miserable limbo of hunger and illness and civil war—a plague visited upon them by the bankruptcy of the policies of all the so-called great powers. The Khmer Rouge no longer rule the country, so their insane massacres and terror have ended, but the country is ruled by outsiders—Cambodia's historical enemies, the Vietnamese. Anti-Vietnamese military groups, including the Khmer Rouge, carry out regular insurgent attacks from bases in remote areas. Civilians are often forced into flight by this civil warfare and the cumulative result is that 250,000 Cambodian refugees now live squalidly, without much hope, along the Thai-Cambodian border.

Thus, the fundamental fact of life for the Cambodians remains what it has been since 1970: their fate and future are in the control of others and their condition is tragedy.

Pran and I have fared much better. When his rotted teeth had been expertly repaired and the malaria erased from his system—and he and Ser Moeun had bought new matching wedding rings, to make up for the one he had bartered for rice—he came to New York to see the people at *The Times* who had been linked to him for nearly a decade but whom he had met only in their cabled messages. It was a time of ebullience and pleasure.

Serious matters had to be resolved, however—a job for Pran, moving arrangements, housing for the family, and schools for the children. Abe Rosenthal, *The Times*'s executive editor, solved the dilemma of what duties would best suit Pran with a command decision. He said Pran would be trained as a photographer, the first time in my memory that any such apprenticeship had been created on the paper. Pran had taken amateur news pictures in Cambodia, as I had, but had no professional skills.

After a trainee stint on the outside with the excellent freelance photographer Peter B. Kaplan, Pran was brought inside to work directly with *The Times*'s staff photographers. Men with large hearts and equally large talents—such as Neal Boenzi, Fred Conrad, and Bill Sauro—gave freely of themselves, even on deadline, and the education of Pran blossomed. He is now a full staff photographer, and his human-interest photos are what he is best known for.

Other New York friends—Mary Kay Gallagher, Linda and Bill Farrell, Jim Clarity, to name a few—helped find a home for Pran's family and place the children in schools. The oldest, Titony, is now a junior at an upstate branch of the State University of New York; Hemkary, the only girl, is a senior in high school; Titonath is a sophomore; and Titonel, the baby at thirteen, is in seventh grade. Ser Moeun, very soon after she had moved the family and settled in, wanted to start earning a salary again; the bank for which she had worked in San Francisco, Wells Fargo, found a place for her in its New York office.

The adjustments have not always been easy, but I have never heard a complaint. The family lives in a warm, rambling house with a backyard on a leafy street in Flatbush that looks more like an all-American small town in Kansas than it does Brooklyn.

While the life of Pran's family is richly bicultural in cuisine and language, their experiences here qualify them as true New Yorkers. They have a mortgage, they have been trapped on broken subway trains, and Pran was mugged one night outside his house as he returned from work. (He was not physically harmed, but the gunman found all the money he had divided into his many shirt, pants, and coat pockets—a habit we developed during the war in Cambodia.)

As for me, I have a new job on *The Times*—as a columnist. I had been the metropolitan editor (city editor, in less fancy language) when Pran escaped from Cambodia, but after doing that for three years, I had a primal urge to get back to writing and said so. The publisher, Arthur Ochs Sulzberger—whose generosity was central in helping support Pran's family while he was missing—responded with a pleasant surprise. He decided to create a column of opinion that had been mulled over for years—a column about New York. So that's what I do now, an essay about New York affairs that appears on the Op-Ed page twice a week.

As in all lives, there have been downs as well as ups. My marriage has ended. I underwent quadruple-bypass heart surgery in the summer of 1983. I have fine children and good friends who have seen me through the occasional difficult times. I think that, like Pran, I am a survivor, and I believe I am a lucky man.

I have found, from my experiences and from the mail I receive, that there are more caring people out there than any of us believe on our average, harassed days. That is a nurturing discovery—if one allows it to seep home.

Neither Pran nor I have left Cambodia behind, nor do we really wish to—although Pran would like his bad dreams to cease. He still has nightmares about his years under the Khmer Rouge. Both he and I keep talking about Cambodia because there are lessons there for us as well as others. This is why we agreed to allow a film to be made about our experiences and about the story of Cambodia. We are very proud of it—for it is honest and faithful to events. It is called *The Killing Fields*, and it powerfully portrays the suffering of the Cambodians and the struggle by Pran, as everyman among his people, to survive.

It also depicts me as a real person, warts and all—which was one of my conditions before agreeing to make the film. It was a personal risk to expose my flaws, to make myself vulnerable in this fashion, but I'm glad I took the risk. The story of this film—the exploitation of a people, the destruction of their culture—is more important than one's fantasy wish to appear heroic and perfect.

Yes, there are times in the film, scenes where my competitive and driven traits are showing, when I get ego twinges and wish more of my gentler side were being displayed. But finally I realize that the movie is heightened reality, not personal or historical exactitude, that the person on the screen is not me but an imagination of me—that the film has a purpose larger than making me look good. It's enough that the film is good.

The letters I get from people who have seen the film tell me this. They tell me that the film is reaching far more people than ever my articles at the time did or could. They tell me that the film is touching people in very personal ways. (In a sense, this reaction is a key reason to have my original article published as a book—so that when *The Killing Fields* is no longer playing at neighborhood theaters, people will still be able to find this story of Cambodia.)

Letters come from people asking how they can help the Cambodian refugees, from people wanting to adopt refugee children, from people moved to donate money and time to relief agencies, from young men and women who want to explain why they have decided to go into social work or enlist in the Peace Corps. What I hear from these voices is that Americans still have a deep need to understand our country's part in the Indochina war, are still looking for something positive out of the darkness of that period.

A mother from San Diego—who had been a flight attendant looking after many refugees on their trips to this country—wrote, after seeing the film, "I was visually unaware of the horrors they left behind. I came home and kissed my two-year-old nonstop. It really made me appreciate all I have, and all the Southeast Asians have left behind. Remember that millions of other people feel as I do and that we have a new respect for these people." A father from Kings Park, New York, wrote similarly: "When I returned from the theater last night, I went into each of my children's rooms (ages four and nine) and whispered—I love you."

I also receive letters from people who just need someone to listen.

A man from Illinois who had volunteered for service in Vietnam in the Coast Guard and who thought he had put the experience entirely behind him ("It was easy for me to forget and get on with my life") says: "Now I feel committed to help in some way. You see, I feel responsible for the situation in Cambodia and need to do something. I know I'm reacting in a moment of emotionalism—however, if I don't react now I may never. It would mean a lot to know you got this and tried to understand how I feel. And for you, Mr. Dith, I am truly sorry and hope you can forgive me and those who served with me for what we have done."

Another veteran wrote of his friendship with a Vietnamese man, Nguyen Van Sung, and his family, from whom he has not heard for over a decade. Of Sung's last letter, sent in 1972, the veteran wrote: "His wife had died giving birth to their fifth child and he was reaching out to me for help. At the end of the letter, he said he knew I couldn't help because my former unit was disbanding and mail service was ending. He thanked me for all I had done, and he told me he would never forget me. Obviously, I have never, never forgotten him and his family. By seeing your story on the screen I relived some of the good times Sung and I had. It helps me live with the guilt of 'leaving them behind.'"

The film has especially touched those new Americans who suffered through its actual events—the surviving Cambodians. "At last I have freedom in a free country that I had wished!" wrote Ngo Tieu Thanh, who has settled in the Bronx. "My life in New York City is still tough because I am the handicap in the wheelchair. However, my mentality and spirit is motivative. I have struggled for my education here until I get into City College. I am very so excited to get into college because I want to have a job in the future in order to support my life— so-called 'independent living.'"

Sarann Reth, a young woman now living in Jaffrey, New Hampshire, said she appreciated the movie even though it made her relive the misery of the Khmer Rouge years. "I saw many things in that movie just like it happened in my life. I worked in the Khmer Rouge labor camp in the mud just like Pran, for four years, from age nine to thirteen."

Vanita Kim, in high school in Oakland, writes of having her memory reluctantly prodded but being pleased, too, because "I want this catastrophe to be known to the public. My father was a professor, and he and my mom and my three brothers were killed by the Communists. Only my sister and I survived. Fortunately, I manipulated to avoid this massacre. Now that I've come to live in U.S., I really had to fight to obtain academic and social equality with my American classmates. But today, I think, I'm fully accepted."

Some Cambodians have written to ask for help in getting

relatives out of the refugee camps in Thailand and into the United States. Both the waiting lists and the bureaucratic obstacles are awesome.

The obstacles are even greater for anyone trying to bring a relative out of Cambodia itself. Pran's mother, sixty-eight years old, still lives in Siem Reap—much too frail to attempt the long journey on foot necessary to make a risky, unofficial exit from Cambodia and unable to get official permission to leave. Why the new government needs to hang on to an ailing, elderly woman escapes me, but Pran and I will keep trying to persuade them to change their minds and let her come to New York and live with Pran. Meanwhile, he and his mother exchange cryptic letters about once a month.

Pran and most of the other Cambodians I know remain in a surprisingly optimistic frame of mind, affirming life not only by being positive one day at a time but also by planning for the future.

Haing Ngor, the Cambodian refugee doctor who plays Pran in the movie, is not an actor. He is, like Pran, a survivor of the Khmer Rouge madness. And also like Pran, he does not allow his memory of man's dark side to take over his existence. Pran and Haing and others like them understand that, incongruous or not, pleasure and tragedy will always exist side by side and that having experienced the latter does not deny one the ability to enjoy.

"You have to have your happy life now," Haing says. "Because when your life is coming to an end, you can't suddenly say, 'Hey, wait a minute, I haven't had my happy life yet, I need a few more years.' It doesn't work that way."

For the refugees in the border camps, not so fortunate as those who have succeeded in getting to a new country and a new start, their search for their piece of a happy life needs everyone's help.

As one American who visited the camps said in a letter to me: "If Cambodia were free, someday they could go back. I fear that that hope is, however, as unrealistic as hoping for freedom in Poland or Latvia. The only alternative is that the West will continue to open its borders to receive those whose past has been taken from them so that they may have a future."